*"Is this your* friends?"

His face brightened; he straightened his shoulders and shuffled closer on the bench. He removed his sunglasses and smiled so that one corner of his mouth tipped up a little more than the other side. Patricia's breath caught. His utterly masculine appeal and the teasing twinkle in his eye would have most women melting at his feet.

Patricia wasn't falling for it. The stakes were too high. What he needed was someone to push him in the right direction and to keep him out of trouble while he reevaluated his life and allowed himself to be touched by God's love.

She cleared her throat. "Yes, I think we can be friends."

He reached forward and picked up a lock of her hair, rubbing it between his fingers. "Or is there something more? I think I see the beginning of a beautiful relationship."

Patricia slapped his hand away and crossed her arms. She wasn't playing some kind of foolish dating game; she didn't play hard-to-get, and she certainly wasn't into his macho routine. "Forget it. I meant as a platonic friendship, and you know it. One false move and it's over. Capiche?"

**GAIL SATTLER** lives in Vancouver, BC (where you don't have to shovel rain), with her husband, three sons, dog, and countless fish, many of whom have names. She writes inspirational romance because she loves happily-ever-afters and believes God has a place in that happy ending. Visit Gail's web site at http://www.gailsattler.com.

**Books by Gail Sattler**

HEARTSONG PRESENTS
HP269—Walking the Dog
HP306—Piano Lessons
HP325—Gone Camping
HP358—At Arm's Length

# My Name
# Is Mike

*Gail Sattler*

*Heartsong Presents*

Dedicated to all the readers who offer me suggestions, especially Lois from Connersville who gave me the idea to write Mike's story. Lois, I wouldn't have thought of this one without you. Thank you.

**A note from the author:**
*I love to hear from my readers! You may correspond with me by writing:*

**Gail Sattler**
**Author Relations**
**PO Box 719**
**Uhrichsville, OH 44683**

ISBN 1-58660-024-9

**MY NAME IS MIKE**

Scripture taken from the HOLY BIBLE: NEW INTERNATIONAL VERSION®. NIV®. Copyright © 1973, 1978, 1984 by International Bible Society. Used by permission of Zondervan Publishing House.

*Cover illustration by Victoria Lisi and Julius.*

PRINTED IN THE U.S.A.

# one

*God grant me the serenity
to accept the things I cannot change,
courage to change the things I can,
and the wisdom to know the difference.*

"My name is Mike, and I'm an alcoholic."

"Hi, Mike," murmured the roomful of people.

Mike Flannigan cleared his throat and scanned the crowd. There were about fifty people in the room.

"This is my first AA meeting, and I'm not really an alcoholic. I'm only doing this because I don't have a choice."

Most people in the crowd smiled wryly.

Mike cleared his throat again, not having received the sympathy he thought he should have. "I was forced to be here by my probation officer."

Mike stopped speaking and scowled at Bruce, expecting Bruce to lose his insipid grin. Instead, Bruce turned around to the crowd with a wide smile and waved. A number of the people in the crowd waved back, more nodded in understanding. Mike couldn't believe it.

He'd seen from the previous two people who stood at the front that nothing was sacred here. Both of them, a man and a woman, had said some very personal things—private types of things that he wouldn't say to his best friend. Yet they'd poured out their hearts to this roomful of people. While it was obvious many knew each other, he could tell many were also strangers or, at best, only casual acquaintances. He vowed he would never do that, and he certainly hadn't expected the group to welcome Bruce.

5

"I'm only here because I got caught drinking and driving. I made a mistake, that was all."

Mike hustled back to his chair; the crowd applauded gently, just as they had for the previous speakers. An older man rose and walked to the podium.

"My name is Claude, and I'm an alcoholic."

"Hi, Claude," the crowd responded.

"I'm not going to give you my usual drunk-a-log tonight. Besides, most of you have heard it before."

The crowd laughed.

"I'm going to tell you about my first meeting. I see we have a few first-timers here tonight, and it got me thinking. Maybe because I'm coming up to my seven-year cake."

Everyone applauded.

Mike leaned to whisper to Bruce. "What's a seven-year cake?"

Bruce leaned toward Mike and whispered back. "It's the anniversary of seven years without a drink. They bring a cake to the meeting, and everyone has a piece. It's a small celebration."

Seven years without a drink. Mike couldn't remember the last time he'd been seven *days* without a drink. Maybe he did drink a little too much, but it was nothing he couldn't handle. He just lost it for one night, he got caught, and that was why he was here.

Claude continued. "I didn't think I had a drinking problem. I was on the brink of losing my job. I stopped getting invitations from my family because I ruined every family gathering. The only friends I had left were drinking buddies, and their friendship depended on when my money ran out. Still, I couldn't go a day without a drink. Then my wife left me because of what my drinking was doing to her and the kids. That's what brought me to my first meeting. I had nowhere to go but up because the next step was straight to hell. Hitting bottom is a different place for each of us, but we all have one. For some it's a job. For some it's money. For some it's personal. The thing that made me stop and take a look at myself was when Michelle left. That was the day I knew I had to change. It was hard, but nothing would have been harder than life alone with only a bottle in an empty apartment for company."

Claude paused, and the crowd remained silent, respecting Claude as he fought with his memories. "You first-timers, think of today, your first meeting. Life gets better from here. Join a twelve-step group. Get in touch with your Higher Power. Go to meetings often, every day if you have to, and mark today on your calendar. Today is the first day of the rest of your life."

The crowd burst into rounds of applause as Claude returned to his chair.

Mike clapped weakly. Claude seemed like a happy guy. He wondered if Claude had got back together with his wife.

Mike listened politely to what the remaining speakers had to say, and when the hour was up, he aimed himself for the door. He didn't care if Bruce was behind him; he would wait for Bruce in the parking lot. He almost made it out when Claude stopped him.

"So when was your last drink, Mike?"

Mike stiffened. "Yesterday." And he was going to have another one the second he got back home.

"Before you take that next drink, think of what you heard today. I look forward to seeing you again soon." He stuffed a piece of paper in Mike's shirt pocket and turned around to talk to someone else.

Fortunately, Bruce was right behind him, and they headed straight for Bruce's car.

Mike stared out the car window the entire trip home without saying a word. He wondered how Claude knew what he was thinking. He didn't have a wife to lose, and since he would one day take over his father's company, his job was set for life.

However, what Claude said about his friends had a note of similarity to it. He tried to think of a single friend who had stood beside him when he'd been arrested. Not one had made any effort to help him. In fact, some of them had laughed.

Only because of Claude's implied suggestion, he would not drink tonight.

He flicked on the television and parked himself on the couch but couldn't sit still. Especially today, he felt the absence of a glass in his hand as he sat alone. Rather than dwell on it, he stomped to the bedroom to change and go to bed early since there was nothing decent on television anyway. When he began to unbutton his shirt, a crumple sounded in his pocket. Inside was the piece of paper Claude had given him. Instead of the AA rhetoric he had expected, it was a simple handwritten note.

> *"Therefore, if anyone is in Christ, he is a new creation;*
> *the old has gone,*
> *the new has come!"*
> *2 Cor. 5:17*

Mike stared at the note. The words *"he is a new creation"* were heavily underlined.

He stared at the paper in his hand. He didn't need to become new. The old Mike was just fine. What he needed was to get some sleep. He threw the paper on the floor and crawled into bed.

❧

Patricia Norbert picked up the ringing phone. "Hello?"

"May I please speak to Bruce?" a shaky baritone voice asked.

"I'm sorry, he's not home. Is there a message?"

"Do you know what time he's going to be back?"

Patricia checked her watch. The caller's tone made her suspect it was one of her brother's probation cases. Bruce's supervisor was constantly telling him not to give out his home number. If it was an emergency, they were supposed to contact the answering service and the message would be forwarded. Again, it appeared Bruce thought differently.

"Not until late. Is there something you need?"

The voice laughed hesitantly. "I need to ask him for an address."

Patricia frowned. Just like their father, Bruce never discussed personal details of his case histories. However, in this case, Bruce had left a note on the fridge for her because he was hoping for a certain call.

"May I ask who's calling?"

"It's Mike. Mike Flannigan."

Patricia rested her finger on the note. "Can you wait for a minute, Mike? Bruce asked me to let him know if you called."

Patricia pulled her cell phone out of her purse, walked into the living room where Mike wouldn't hear what she said, and dialed Bruce's cell number.

"Bruce? It's Patty. Mike called, just like you said, and he wants to talk to you."

"He probably feels the need for another AA meeting. I had a feeling he might, and that's good. But I can't get out of here for another hour, and the meeting starts before then. The address is on the fridge. I guess he'll have to take a cab because he lost his license. I wanted to take him just to make sure he went, but I can't. Oops. I gotta go."

Patricia didn't know much about Alcoholics Anonymous except for what Bruce had told her. Evidently, the group's history started in 1935 as a Bible study but had been watered down in its spiritual content to include more people who needed help. Although she failed to understand how anyone could let alcohol strip a person's common sense and dignity, she respected any organization that helped people get their lives back together. She also knew that many people found Christ through the AA program.

If Bruce considered Mike worth breaking the rules for, it was all Patricia needed to know. She walked back into the kitchen and pulled the note off the fridge.

She checked the time and picked up the phone. "Mike? Bruce left the address and time right here, but the meeting starts in half an hour. If you have to wait for a cab, you'll be late for the meeting. Bruce thought it was important for you to go, so I can take you. I've got your address. I'll be there in ten minutes." Patricia hung up before Mike could reply, locked up Bruce's house, and was on her way.

Mike's house surprised her. Due to his being one of her brother's cases, she hadn't expected an executive home. The large house's stark white stucco exterior contrasted elegantly with the deep red Spanish villa-style shingles and shutters. Tall trees graced the professionally landscaped property, and the driveway, rather than being plain cement, was cobblestone.

Whoever Mike was, Mike had more money than she'd ever have.

Patricia knocked. A man answered the door. He was tall, and she guessed him to be in his mid-thirties. He wore his dark brown hair in a short, stylish cut which emphasized his chis-eled features. His clothes fit him so perfectly she suspected they were tailor-made. While he wasn't movie star handsome, he was better than average. Patricia wondered if he was ill because he was pale, and his hands were slightly shaky.

She straightened and patted her purse strap on her shoulder. "I'm looking for Mike Flannigan."

His face paled even more. "Are you Bruce's wife?"

"No, I'm his sister, Patty. Are you Mike? I'm here to take you to the meeting."

He nodded and glanced at his wristwatch. "I guess we should go then."

She backed up a step while he grabbed a waist-length leather jacket from beside the door and locked up.

Conversation in the car was stilted, which Patricia could

understand because of the awkward situation. When the usual pleasantries were done, she drove to the address on Bruce's note in silence.

They arrived at an older church building in a well-established neighborhood. Bruce's instructions said that the room they were looking for was in the basement, but they wouldn't have needed further instructions. The noise would have led them to the right room. The cloud of cigarette smoke was another dead giveaway. They arrived with minutes to spare, so they hurried in.

Once inside, they were welcomed openly. When Patricia greeted newcomers at church, she always asked a few simple questions, such as where they were from and if someone else whom she would help locate had invited them. However, no questions were asked, not even their names, which Patricia thought quite odd but probably suited the *Anonymous* part of the name *Alcoholics Anonymous*.

They were shown to the coffee table at the back and told to help themselves quickly before the meeting started. Patricia didn't take any coffee because it was evening, but Mike poured a large cup for himself, and they quickly found two seats together near the back.

A man stepped up to the podium and welcomed everyone present. With little preamble, he introduced another man, by first name only, as the first speaker. Mike sat stiff as a board beside her, cradling the Styrofoam cup with both hands in his lap.

Patricia had some experience with a few of the members of the congregation coming from alcoholic backgrounds, but nothing would have prepared her for the things the speakers said at this meeting.

The first speaker told of how when he was drinking, his wife hid or dumped all the liquor in the house. She timed him from when he left work to make sure he didn't stop at the bar, yet by the time he arrived home, he'd had plenty to drink, and no one could figure out how he got it. The man now laughed at himself, disgusted by how pathetic he was. He had devised a way to store his liquor in the windshield wiper container under the hood of his car and drank on the way home through a tube he'd run to the driver's seat. Now that he'd been sober for a number of years, he could laugh at himself, but he shared with the group that he wished he could be as creative on the job and with his family as he had been when he was desperately finding ways to get enough to drink every day.

A woman told of how she thought drinking with the right crowd would further her career. She blamed management favoritism for passing her up for every promotion until one day she took a hard look at herself from a hospital bed. In what was supposed to be a dignified moment, she had been so drunk she tripped in her high-heeled shoes and broke her leg. Confined to the hospital for a couple of days, and without access to alcohol, she had time and a clear head to think about the direction her life was going. She discovered that she no longer associated with those who should have been her peers. The right crowd gradually stopped hanging around with her because her personality changed when she drank, until the only people who would put up with her were those she never would have associated with five years ago.

Patricia fought back tears at the testimony of a man who told of how his wife finally left him because of his drinking. His wife had begun the process of a court battle to limit his visitation rights to his children, but for the time, he still had his two teenaged children every second weekend. One day, his daughter, knowing her father was drunk again, decided to walk home alone late at night rather than call him for a ride home. The girl was brutally attacked.

Patricia couldn't understand how people could let their lives be so controlled by drink, but at the same time, she couldn't deny that it happened.

She was pleasantly surprised to hear the meeting end with

everyone repeating the Lord's prayer.

At the close of the meeting, she turned to Mike. She didn't know what it was he had done to have Bruce assigned to him as his probation officer, nor did she know how bad his drinking problem was, only that Bruce thought it was important for Mike to attend this session. As she opened her mouth to speak, her words stuck in her throat. Mike's face was expressionless, hard and closed. He stood quickly, crushing the empty cup as he rose.

"I've got to get out of here," he mumbled.

They had almost made it to the door when an older man stopped them.

"Mike! Good to see you again!" The man pumped Mike's hand and patted Mike on the shoulder with his other hand.

Mike didn't respond. His face tightened, and his whole body stiffened.

The man turned to Patricia. "I'm Claude, and I met Mike yesterday at the meeting on Royal Street. It's good to see him here." He released the handshake, but one hand remained firm on Mike's shoulder. Patricia could see that however Mike was raised, he had manners, because even though it was obvious Mike was not comfortable, he allowed himself to remain captive to Claude's firm hand still on his shoulder.

"I went to a meeting every day for many months when I first joined AA. I knew myself well enough not to risk going home to an empty apartment, because it would only remind me of what I didn't want to face. I knew until I could get a handle on my new life that if I spent night after night alone, I would end up drinking again. Are you two, uh, together?"

Patricia didn't want to embarrass Mike because she didn't know any details of his life, or his case, so she didn't want to tell the man the only thing she knew about Mike was his name and address. "Yes, we're together," she mumbled.

Claude nodded. "It's so noisy here. How about if we go out for coffee, to talk away from the crowd. Mostly, the smoke here bothers me. You don't smoke, do you?"

Patricia shook her head, and she was relieved to see that Mike did the same.

"Good. Let's go to the donut place down the street. I'll see you there." He turned and left before either of them had a chance to decline.

"What do you want to do?" Patricia asked Mike, checking her watch instead of looking at his face. "I've got plenty of time."

"I don't care," he mumbled. "You're driving."

She wondered if Mike were always this surly but chose to give him the benefit of the doubt.

Fortunately it took only a few minutes to drive to the donut shop, and they pulled into the parking lot at the same time as Claude. The girl behind the counter appeared to know him well as a regular customer, and they were soon seated in a corner booth.

&

"Well, Mike, I'm not going to ask if you're enjoying your first meetings, because I sure didn't when I first started." Claude paused to chuckle, then poured some sugar into his coffee.

Mike didn't see anything funny. He'd never been so uncomfortable in his life. The only reason he was there was as a condition of his probation. While it was true that he probably did drink a little too much, he didn't have a problem. He certainly wasn't an alcoholic—he never drank before lunchtime, and he was no skid-row wino. He had a nice home and a good job, and he never drank cheap booze just to get drunk. He only drank the best. After all, he could afford it. The only reason he felt shaky and on edge was because he was probably coming down with the flu.

"It looks like you've never been to a meeting before, have you, Patty?"

She smiled weakly. "No. Is it that obvious?"

Claude nodded and smiled. "Oh, yes."

Mike looked at Bruce's sister. She wasn't hard on the eyes. She was just what he considered the right height for a woman, about five and a half feet, and she was kinda cute. He figured she was about thirty. Her light brown hair was slightly wavy and hung loose, accenting her wide eyes and pouty little mouth. What he liked best was her blue eyes, large and expressive, taking in everything around them in wide-eyed fascination. She was different from the other women he knew. Patty Norbert's expressive eyes hid nothing. He could tell she was frightened by the more aggressive people in the room, and most of all, she obviously felt out of place. It was as if she had the words "I don't belong here" stamped across her forehead.

Most of the women he'd seen at the meetings had a hard-bitten edge to them, which he could understand. It seemed a good number of the people there had been through a major trauma or had some kind of hard-luck story, which was why they were there. Patty had been even more uncomfortable than he was, and it bothered him that she was there because of him.

Mike lowered his head and stared into his cup. At any other time, he could have appreciated getting to know a woman, but tonight all he could think of was the things he'd heard.

"Well, Mike. What brings you to AA? Last night you said you got caught drinking and driving."

He looked up at Claude and Patty, both of whom were studying him. He could have easily snowed Claude, but since his connection to Patty was through her brother, his probation officer, she would know there was more to the story.

He looked straight into Patty's eyes, her beautiful blue eyes—innocent eyes. He didn't know why she had come with him, but he didn't want her there. If Bruce couldn't accompany him to any of the mandatory twice-weekly AA meetings, he would rather go alone.

"It's a condition of my probation, and I'm going to use it as part of a plea bargain for when my court case comes up."

He noticed she blinked and stiffened. That was good.

"I had a little bit too much to drink one night, and had an accident. I didn't want to take a Breathalyzer test, so I took off, but they caught me. It's just a first offense, and my lawyer told me that I'll probably get off with a slap on the wrist or a very short sentence if I behave and go to AA meetings like a good boy."

Her eyes widened even more, and a light gasp escaped. "You drove away? What if the people in the other car were hurt?"

Mike stared down into his cup. It hadn't bothered him at the time. All he'd thought about in his drunken state was his own skin. But now that it was over, the guilt was starting to get to him. "It was only one guy in the car," he muttered, not looking up. "He wasn't hurt too badly. I found out he only had a broken arm or something." His lawyer had told him that the man couldn't work for a few months because of that broken arm, but Mike figured it wasn't so bad. It would be a little vacation, paid for by the man's insurance, and he'd be getting a new car out of the deal.

Patty said nothing, which was fine with Mike.

Claude didn't even blink. "So you've been charged with DWI and leaving the scene. What did your friends say?"

He stared up at Claude. "Nothing. It's not their problem. It's mine."

"Nice friends you've got."

Mike didn't want to think of his friends and how much they'd let him down. None of them would lend him the money to make bail, and they were all too drunk to come and pick him up from the police station. He had had to call his dad, who wasn't pleased to have his thirty-three-year-old son call in the middle of the night, asking to get him out of trouble and pay his bail.

And tonight, when he needed someone to talk to after all

he'd been through, most of his friends chose, instead, to go to the club like any other night. The rest of them had gone to Trevor's house where they could get drunker quicker and partake of substances they couldn't be seen using in the bar. He wasn't in the mood for that, especially not so soon after someone had been hurt because of him. For a while, he had been tempted, but a comment he'd heard at the first meeting stuck in his mind—that drinking had become the most important thing in the speaker's life. Mike had been reaching for a drink at the time that he recalled the comment.

It made him think, maybe he did have a bit of a drinking problem. And that was why he'd called Bruce to take him to another meeting. The conditions of his probation stated a minimum of two meetings a week. Bruce had encouraged him to do more, and last night Claude had said he'd been to a meeting every day when he first started going.

He gulped down the last of the coffee, then thunked the cup to the table. "I can handle this on my own."

As soon as the words left his mouth, he knew he'd made a mistake. A change came over Patty. The shock in her face softened, her eyes widened, and her mouth opened slightly in the saddest expression he'd ever seen. She felt sorry for him, and that was the last thing he wanted. He didn't need anyone to feel sorry for him. He had gotten into this mess himself, and he was going to get himself out.

Thankfully, he didn't have to say anything. Claude also lowered his cup to the table and checked his watch. "This has been good, but I've got to get up early for work tomorrow. What about you two?"

Patty checked her watch as well. "Yes, I work as the secretary for our church, and sometimes my hours are flexible but not this week. I've got to be in early tomorrow morning."

Mike stood. "I've got to be at work in the morning, too." He wasn't going to tell them that he worked for his father's company, and he showed up for work at whatever time he got himself together in the morning. He was the office manager, and it was no one's business what time he got there.

They left together, and Mike followed Patty to her car. On the way home, they passed a large church, which she pointed out as where she worked. He'd known a few people who went to church over the years, but he'd never met someone who actually worked for one.

This time, they actually talked during the drive home. He found Patty pleasant and easy to talk to. He'd meant to shock her with the reason her brother was his probation officer, but now that she knew, she wasn't judgmental, nor did she turn her nose up at him. She just talked to him like everything was normal.

Mike needed normal. All that his friends did was laugh at him for being stupid and getting caught. His family, especially his father, was furious, and even though Mike hated to admit it, rightfully so. And then, at work, he knew everyone was whispering behind his back, and it hurt.

Too soon, they were stopped in front of his house. He politely thanked Patty and went inside. She'd been nice to give him a ride when he needed it and, after all the awkwardness was over, she'd been quite pleasant to talk to. Most of all, she hadn't snubbed him or talked down to him as one of her brother's low-life cases but treated him like a normal human being. He appreciated that right now more than she would ever know.

Since Mike would never see her again, he wouldn't have the opportunity to thank her properly. Therefore, Mike decided to send her flowers in the morning. He didn't know where she lived, but he did know where she worked.

# two

Patricia sat on the secluded park bench, enjoying the warm sunshine. She smiled as the little brown squirrel snatched the piece of bread from her fingers. It ran a safe distance away and held the morsel between its tiny paws. While it ate, it kept a watchful eye on everything around, trusting nothing, not even her.

Just like Mike.

Patricia sighed. She couldn't get him out of her mind.

She turned her head briefly to glance at the church. She always enjoyed taking her lunch break outside at the park next to the church, but today she needed the escape more than ever.

He'd sent her flowers. She'd never had flowers delivered to her personally. She'd often been involved with receiving flowers and setting them out for occasions and special services, but no one had ever sent them just for her.

The only thing on the note was the word "Thanks," and his name. She wasn't sure if it was a simple thank you for the ride, or for something more.

He'd said almost nothing to her until Claude took them out to the donut shop and asked Mike for details as to why he went to the meetings. She knew Mike's answer was meant to intimidate her and make her back off. She'd been in ministry long enough and counseled enough people to know what he was trying to do.

What had surprised her was the way he'd responded to her in the car during the drive home. She'd only meant to be friendly, recognizing that he felt abandoned by his friends and family. She'd kept the conversation light and carefree, and he'd responded. After he began to relax, she'd asked him a few questions and listened to his opinion, to show him that he had value as a human being. Once he let his guard down, he'd been very pleasant to talk to, and she'd actually enjoyed their conversation.

Apparently, when he wanted to, Mike could be quite charming. If it hadn't been for the fact that she knew he had a severe drinking problem, and that he'd tried to run from the law in an effort to save his own skin, and that drinking and driving appeared to be a habit of his, and that he had tried to manipulate her, she might have fallen for it. She also had no doubt that he was used to getting his own way.

As interesting as she found Mike, she knew it wasn't smart to get involved in any of Bruce's cases, especially this one. Just like she wouldn't get involved when her father was counseling someone, unless she was specifically asked, she was not going to get further involved with Mike, especially since Mike wasn't a Christian. She couldn't miss his disbelief when she told him she worked for the church. Still, something about him fascinated her, although it was probably because her heart always went out to those in need, and she could see he needed a friend, badly.

The little squirrel finished his bread and approached cautiously for more. Patricia moved very slowly so as not to scare him, and when he took it, she remained bent over, waiting until he was far enough away not to be frightened when she moved to sit up.

Suddenly, the squirrel darted away. She sighed and flopped back on the bench. She'd thought the little squirrel was becoming more used to her because, unless it rained, over the past few weeks she had fed it almost every day.

"Hi, Patty. Mind if I join you?"

Patricia screeched, and all the bread flew out of her hands. At the same time as she turned her head to place the semi-familiar baritone voice, Mike stepped into her line of vision.

He was wearing sunglasses, pleated dress slacks, and the same leather jacket as last night, over a pale blue dress shirt. His cheeks were slightly pink from being outside in the breeze, and his hair was pleasantly mussed. The combination gave him a roguish appeal.

She pressed one hand to her pounding heart. "Mike! You scared me. What are you doing here?"

He smiled as he scanned the ground, noting the scattered pieces of bread. "I just needed to go for a walk, and before I knew it, I was here. May I sit down?"

She knew his home was a fair distance away, not what she would call a leisurely walking distance. She wondered how he got there. "Of course you can have a seat." She shuffled over to give him room. She knew Mike also had a job, yet they were miles from downtown or any industrial estates. She knew he wasn't driving, and again wondered how he got there.

"This is a nice little spot. I went inside the church, but the pastor told me you were on your lunch break, and that I'd find you here." He sat beside her, leaned back, rested one elbow on the back of the bench, crossed one ankle over the opposite knee, and smiled.

She stared into his face. She couldn't see his eyes behind the sunglasses, but even with them, he was quite a handsome man. Different from last night, today he oozed confidence and poise, and he was even more attractive when he smiled.

"I was just feeding the squirrel," she said, looking past the bread on the ground, and into the trees. The squirrel was gone, and she doubted it would be back today. She checked her watch. "It's almost time for me to get back to work."

At her words, which she had meant only as a hint that she couldn't stay outside much longer, Mike's expression changed. His smile dropped, he sat straight, then slumped. Resting his elbows on his knees, he picked off the sunglasses and buried his face in his palms. "I'm not going back to work.

My dad fired me today."

"Oh. . . Mike. . . I'm so sorry."

He shook his head, not removing his hands from his face, his sunglasses dangling from his fingers. "I shouldn't have come here, but I needed someone to talk to."

Her heart went out to him. If he had no one else he could turn to, then she would stay with him on the park bench and let him talk. If she was late getting back to work, she knew her father would understand, and she knew Bruce would also understand her involvement, since it was Mike who had sought her out, not the other way around. She could always do the church bulletin tonight, or come in Saturday to finish it, although she hated leaving things until the last minute. However, people were more important than the bulletin. She waited in silence to let Mike continue when he was ready.

"I don't understand. Dad has always stuck up for me and helped me out before. He paid my bail and made arrangements to have my car released from the impound yard. And since I can't drive it, he also arranged to have it fixed. Everything was fine, just like usual. But today, when I told him I went to another AA meeting, and without my probation officer this time, he changed. He told me what a disappointment I was, and that my services were no longer required. He told me to clean out my desk and get out."

He paused to draw in a ragged breath. "You know the first thing I wanted to do? My first thought was how bad I wanted to go home and have a drink. I was desperate for the quickest way to get home. And then I caught myself. My first meeting, one of the speakers said he knew he had a problem when he admitted that the most important thing in his life was getting that next drink. And that's all I could think of. The quickest way to go home and drink myself into oblivion. So I came here instead."

Patricia sat still, watching Mike, and thinking. If she understood correctly, his father's company was apparently quite large and successful, judging from the way he was dressed and the exterior of his expensive home which she had already seen. From what Mike had said yesterday, this was the first time he'd been arrested, but from his comment about his relationship with his father, it sounded like this was not the first time he'd been in trouble.

In her experience with counseling, she'd seen many times when a parent or spouse, by excusing wrong behavior, covering it up, and even making excuses for it, unwittingly encouraged it to continue. She suspected Mike's father was such a person.

However, she couldn't understand why Mike's admission that he had started going to AA meetings would cause the support to stop. In what seemed an ongoing pattern, Mike finally admitted to having a problem and was actively doing something about it, even though it had initially been forced on him as a condition of his probation.

Patricia thought it was a tremendous step forward for Mike to want to talk about going to the meetings, now that he admitted he needed help. Help he apparently wasn't going to get from his friends or family.

"Do you believe in God, Mike?"

He sat up and looked back at her, squinting in the sunlight. "Yeah, I believe in God," he mumbled. "I've even been to church a number of times with, uh, well, someone I used to know."

"Going to church isn't the same as believing in God."

"I said I believed."

"But in what? Look at all of this," she swept one hand through the air, encompassing the serene park with the stately church building behind them, the magnificent trees in front of them, and the beauty of the brilliant blue sky above. "Acknowledging that a supreme God created all of this, as well as you and me, and knowing it up here," she tapped her index finger to her head, "isn't the same as knowing that this

same God loves you, no matter what you've done. You've got
to know it in here," she pressed her palms to her heart. "God
loves you enough to have sent His Son, Jesus, to take the
punishment for your sins, and the slate can be wiped clean.
That's what you've got to believe. God can help you over-
come this, if you let Him."

Mike blew out a breath of air tersely between light lips.
"What is this? *Touched by an Angel?* Should I call you
Monica? Are you going to start glowing?" He put his sun-
glasses back on and scowled.

Patricia sucked in a deep breath and let it out slowly. She
refused to let his sarcasm affect her. He was hurting, so he
was striking out at her in a misguided attempt to deal with
what was happening to him.

"You blew it, Mike, and you blew it real bad. And now
you've got to do something about it."

"Well. That was certainly what I came all this way to hear."

Patricia crossed her arms over her chest. "You know that
it's time to take a good look at yourself and do something
before you ruin your whole life."

"Thanks for the encouragement."

"I'm telling you this as a friend, Mike."

"My friends would feel sorry for me, not rub my face in it."

"I'm not rubbing your face in it. If I saw one of my friends
starting to get involved in something wrong or harmful, I
would say something. And I trust that if I started to do something bad, I know many people would say nothing, but my
real friends would tell me I was doing something wrong, even
though I might hate them for it. They would try to steer me in
the right direction, no matter what the cost, and I'd do the
same for them. That's true friendship."

"Is this your way of saying you want to be friends?" His
face brightened; he straightened his shoulders and shuffled
closer on the bench. He removed his sunglasses and smiled so
that one corner of his mouth tipped up a little more than the

other side. Patricia's breath caught. His utterly masculine appeal and the teasing twinkle in his eye would have most women melting at his feet.

Patricia wasn't falling for it. The stakes were too high. What he needed was someone to push him in the right direction and to keep him out of trouble while he reevaluated his life and allowed himself to be touched by God's love.

She cleared her throat. "Yes, I think we can be friends."

He reached forward and picked up a lock of her hair, rubbing it between his fingers. "Or is there something more? I think I see the beginning of a beautiful relationship."

Patricia slapped his hand away and crossed her arms. She wasn't playing some kind of foolish dating game, she didn't play hard-to-get, and she certainly wasn't into his macho routine. "Forget it. I meant as a platonic friendship, and you know it. One false move and it's over. Capiche?"

"Capiche." He grinned, which made her doubt his sincerity, but she had to take him at his word, such as it was. "So, how would you like to cement our friendship by going out for dinner with me? Just to talk. And then maybe we can go out somewhere afterwards. It's Friday night. I never sit home alone on Friday night. You wouldn't want to be the one to cause me to fall into temptation to start drinking, would you?"

Patricia narrowed her eyes. "I'll join you for dinner, but don't read anything into it. If we go out anywhere else, it's going to be to another AA meeting."

His smile dropped to a frown. "You're kidding, right?"

"Wrong. If you want to go out for dinner, fine, but only if you go to another meeting after." A meeting where she knew they would see Claude. Claude had slipped her his phone number in the parking lot of the donut shop when Mike wasn't looking. After she'd mentioned at the coffee shop last night that she worked for the church, Claude whispered to her that he was a Christian, too, and that he wanted to help Mike. Between Bruce and Claude, Mike would be in good hands.

Tonight, however, it was up to her to take Mike to the AA meeting, because she knew Bruce had a committee meeting.

He smiled again. "Okay, you win."

Patricia stood, being very obvious about checking her watch. "Oh, there's one more thing. I'm way behind since I'm so late getting back from lunch. If you really want me to join you for dinner, you've got to do my filing." She smiled as sweetly and convincingly as she could.

He leaned back on the bench, crossed his ankles, and linked his fingers behind his head. At his broad smile, a dimple appeared in his left cheek. "You're kidding, right?"

"Wrong. If I'm going to get out on time, I need help. Besides, unless you call a cab, you don't have a way of getting home. You're stuck here until I take you home, so you might as well do something constructive."

"The pastor won't mind?"

"He won't mind at all." Above all, she couldn't let Mike go home, at least not yet. Her father would understand that Mike needed something to do to keep his mind off his troubles until he got a handle on things. "You can start by doing some photo copying, then sort and file clippings and notes for future sermon topics, and then you can file the week's receipts."

He shrugged his shoulders, and thankfully followed her inside without protest.

&bull;

Mike dutifully did what he was told, but he watched Patty constantly out of the corner of his eye.

The woman was sharp. Usually he had women eating out of his hand, but not her. He knew this time he wasn't exactly a prime catch, considering the reason they'd met in the first place. She made it more than plain that he wasn't going to win her heart by mere sympathy, either. Not that he wanted her to feel sorry for him: that was the last thing he wanted.

The first time he met her, he thought she was shy and reserved, but when he met her on her own turf, she stood her ground and called it like she saw it. More than anything, she made him think.

He tucked the last receipt into the folder and closed the filing cabinet drawer, then stood back to watch her work. The woman was organized and efficient but at the same time, warm and friendly when she answered the phone. Likewise, she radiated sensitivity when someone wandered in to ask a question or arrived for an appointment with one of the pastors or the church counselor.

He could see that everyone liked her. He liked her, too. However, the fact that she was his probation officer's sister complicated the issue.

He'd always thought someone who worked in a church would be more subservient, but he was wrong on that one. She could dish it right back as well as take it. The way she showed up on his doorstep to take him to the AA meeting without being asked should have given him the first indication of what he was up against. He'd always thought he picked up on people quickly, but he could now admit that when he'd met her for the first time, his brain had been too foggy to process everything clearly. She'd only been quiet and demure because she'd been out of her element, and he hadn't seen it until now.

Mike watched Patty, busily typing up the church's Sunday bulletin. She was just as focused at work as she had been at the AA meeting. While at work, she worked with all her concentration on the papers in front of her. She occasionally glanced up at the computer screen as she typed. Not once did she look at him, as much as he wanted her to.

Mike leaned back, resting his elbows on the top of the filing cabinet. "I'm all done. Got any more urgent and critical tasks for me? Pencils to sharpen? Paper clips to sort?"

She stopped typing and straightened the stack of papers in front of her. "Everything I've given you needed to be done. And all jobs, however insignificant they appear, are important."

Mike snorted. "Oh. Spare me. I don't give the kids fresh out of school the menial junk you've dumped on me."

She folded her hands and rested them on the base of her keyboard. "Have you always had such a bad attitude?"

"I don't have a bad attitude. You're just bossy."

"I'm not bossy. I'm an efficient adjudicator."

"You're bossy, and you're enjoying it, too."

"I didn't give you anything that I wasn't prepared to do myself. But now all I've got left is the bulletin, which you can't help me with." She tilted her mouth and closed one eye, no doubt thinking of some other meaningless task to keep him occupied. Part of him was amused at her attempts to keep him busy, but something deep inside appreciated what she was trying to do, as much as he hated to admit it.

He actually found it funny that it was so easy to figure out what she was trying to do. The woman was transparent. Every emotion and every thought was written on her face. He would bet she never played Poker, because if she did, she would be lousy at it.

"I really don't have any other work that you can do, so I'm going to give you something else." She opened her drawer and pulled out a Bible.

Mike cringed.

She flipped it open about three-quarters of the way through and handed it to him. "I want you to start reading. This is the book of Matthew, the start of the New Testament. Start at verse eighteen. Do you have a Bible at home?"

"I said I'd been to church before. I didn't say I was a Bible scholar."

"You don't have to be a Bible scholar to read it. Besides, Bruce told me that the AA program is based on biblical principles, so, therefore, you should know something about the Bible. And that can only happen by reading it."

"I don't believe this," he grumbled.

At her answering scowl, he broke out into a wide grin and

held the Bible to his heart. "But for you, I'd do anything."

Patty rolled her eyes. "Give it a rest. This, you don't do for me. You do it for yourself. Now sit down and start reading. I have work to do."

# three

"This wasn't what I meant when I suggested dinner."

Patricia fluttered her eyelashes and smiled sweetly. "But I love this place."

She tried not to laugh at his answering scowl. She knew he wanted to go someplace that would have been suitable for a date, so she picked the place that was the furthest extreme from date-worthy she could think of. Sir Henry's Fish and Chip Palace fit the bill perfectly. "I can't remember the last time I had fish and chips." Sir Henry's was less a restaurant and more a combination of take-out and a glorified lunch counter. Most importantly, they didn't serve alcohol.

"There are only four tables and a counter. They don't even have menus. This place is a hole in the wall."

"I like to think of it as cozy."

He grumbled something she couldn't quite make out, which was probably for the best.

"Quit complaining, and let's order. We don't have much time."

They looked up at the menu board, told Henry what they wanted, and sat at a table after Mike insisted on paying, which she knew he would. It was another reason she'd picked Sir Henry's. The food was cheap.

"When Henry calls our number, we're supposed to go pick it up, but he'll probably bring it to our table."

Mike harumphed. "Call our number? We're the only ones in here!"

"Shhhh! Not so loud! They get mostly people taking it home to eat, but we don't have time for that today. You must admit the place has character."

Faded red-and-white-checkered curtains hung cafe-style on tarnished brass rods with huge ornate ends, making her think they had been the same ones Henry had up in 1973 when he opened the place. The marred tabletops were stained, but always clean, likewise the old wooden chairs, most of which sported different fabrics of different generations on the padded seats. What the place lacked in furniture, it made up for in photographs. Every space on the wall held a framed photograph either depicting the restaurant over the years, such as a faded blown-up shot of Henry's opening day, or some part of Jolly Ol' England, which had been snapped by Henry himself or sent to him by a relative still living there.

Mike rolled his eyes. "Yeah. Right. Character."

Since the place was small, they heard the sizzle of the deep fryer. She didn't normally eat such greasy fare, but she made the exception for Sir Henry's, since the food was so good. "You're really going to enjoy this. I promise."

His scowl turned into a smile. "You know, for some reason, I believe you. I don't know why, but I do."

Patricia chose to accept his comment as a compliment, whether or not that was how it was meant. She smiled, rested her elbows on the table, and said nothing.

Mike studied a photograph of Big Ben, then folded his hands on the table and turned to her. "Before we go any further, I want to apologize. I'm not usually so miserable. I don't know what's come over me. I can only use the excuse that I'm still trying to sort out what's happened, and I haven't been myself lately. And I don't know why I'm talking to you like this. You seem to bring it out in me."

"Honesty is always the best policy."

He shook his head. "Not if I'm trying to impress you."

"You're not supposed to be trying to impress me. You're supposed to be working your way through this and straightening out your life. I can only imagine how difficult this has been for you." She also suspected it was going to get harder before it got better, as that was usually the case when some-one started working through such a long-term problem, espe-cially when there was an addiction or compulsive behavior involved. "Besides, your charm is lost on me. I want you to work on whatever it takes to clean yourself up and move for-ward with your life. All I want to be is friends."

When their dinner was ready, Henry couldn't leave the long line-up of cars at the drive-thru window, so Mike picked up their order at the counter when Henry called out their number. Mike both grumbled and joked at the same time about their still being the only ones inside as he placed the tray on the table, which Patricia thought quite endearing. In a way she couldn't quite figure out, he had a charm about him that naturally gravitated people toward him. Fortunately, she was immune.

She bowed her head and folded her hands on the table, and Mike followed her lead, waiting as she prepared herself to pray.

"Thank You, Father God, for this day of new beginnings and for Your wisdom as You guide us through the path You've laid out before us. Thank You, also, for this food and for new friends to share it with. Amen."

"Amen," Mike mumbled.

He didn't complain about her praying in a public restau-rant, which would have probably been more public if they weren't the only people there besides the owner. Still, Patricia chose to interpret his acquiescence to her prayers as encouraging.

Mike took his first bite cautiously, paused, then smiled. "As much as I hate to admit it, this is pretty good."

Patricia smiled back and agreed. Throughout dinner, Mike playfully complained about everything around them, but she noticed he ate every morsel in front of him.

When she was done, she dropped her napkin on top of what she couldn't finish. "I'm stuffed. We'd better go."

Mike checked his watch. "Yes. I don't want to walk in at the last minute again."

On the drive to the meeting, Mike compared what he saw as every shortcoming of Sir Henry's with the finer points of where he would have taken her, had they gone where he wanted. He also made it plain that at the restaurant of his choice, dinner tonight would have been a date, which was exactly what Patricia wanted to avoid.

By now, even though she didn't know him very well, she easily figured out that Mike used his easy charm to his advantage. It wasn't hard to see that he knew women in general were easily attracted to him. She also had no doubt he'd used the same technique to get himself out of trouble. Often.

It made Patricia very much aware of the sheltered life she'd led. Sometimes she appreciated it; sometimes she didn't. In times like this, she did. She knew that men like Mike left trails of heartache in their wake, and she had been spared from the experience so far. At thirty, she had dated before but never had what she would call a serious relationship. She had carefully dated only well-grounded Christian men; never *bad-boy* types like Mike.

The downside of her love life was that, even though it was unintentional, most men had been intimidated by her father, many having future dreams of ministry themselves. While naturally she could share in their excitement, she often felt used, or set on a pedestal as her father's daughter, neither of which she wanted out of the man who would one day be her husband.

This meeting was also in a church building. Just as they turned into the parking lot, Mike spoke up.

"You know, I really don't know anything about you, other than you work at your church. I guess you also attend there, and stuff."

Patricia smiled. "All my life, except when I went to Bible college."

"Bible college, huh? I guess that shouldn't surprise me. Do

you live close to the church, too?"

"Yes, I do. But not close enough to walk. If you're wondering why I had my car."

"No, not at all. Just wondering, that's all. The first time I talked to you, you were at Bruce's house."

She couldn't imagine why where she lived would concern him. "I was just borrowing his computer that night because I don't have a scanner. I'm not there often. Come on, we should go in."

"How exactly did you know about this meeting? Did you talk to Bruce? Is he putting a note in my file that I'm here?"

"No, I haven't spoken to Bruce. If you want to tell him, fine; I can vouch for you. Claude told me about this last night in the donut shop parking lot."

Mike's step faltered. "Claude? Do you know him? Does he go to your church or something?"

Patricia shook her head as Mike caught up, and they entered the building together. "Nope. Never met him before last night. I thought you knew him."

It was Mike's turn to shake his head. "I only met him at my first meeting. He slipped me a note with a Bible verse on it. I guess there must be quite a few Christians in the program."

"That's what Bruce says."

Sure enough, they hadn't been in the meeting room long when Claude appeared. Without being prompted, he sat beside Mike, and the meeting began.

As happened at the previous meeting, Patricia listened to everyone share their stories. A couple of people went quite in-depth with personal testimonies, but most of them grazed the surface of their own stories while they shared words of wisdom with the group. One man in particular had the entire crowd in stitches. His delivery was hilarious, but his real message wasn't funny at all. Despite what had happened in his life, this man named Gerry had a wonderful attitude, and she wondered if Mike would be able to look back on his life some day and be able to laugh like that at the stupid things he'd done.

At the close of the meeting, they remained seated.

Claude slid his chair so it was turned toward both of them. "In a few weeks, it's going to be my seven-year cake, and this is my home group. I would be honored if both of you would be here to share it with me. I'd also like you to meet my wife, Michelle. She's going to be here for the occasion. The only times she comes to meetings is when it's an anniversary cake for me."

Before she had time to think about it, Mike pumped Claude's hand. "We'd love to come, and we're honored to be asked. Right, Patty?"

She hadn't realized they would have been considered a couple. Patricia wondered how she could let Claude know they weren't as together as they appeared. "Uh. . .of course. . . we'd be delighted."

Claude beamed. "Great! I'll be waiting to see you there."

Mike didn't smile. "You know, today I'd swear that some of the thoughts and feelings of some of the people who got up to speak were taken right out of my own head. I've got to ask, if you don't mind telling me, once you went to your first meeting, did you go back and drink for a while?"

"No, I didn't. Since I went to my first meeting, I haven't touched a drop of liquor."

"Not a single drink? Never? How did you do it?"

"The first thing I did was get rid of all the booze. All of it. Even when Michelle and I got back together, nothing was saved. Not even for when company came over. Nothing was saved or served on holidays, or any day, in our house, after that. Even the bottle of wine Michelle kept for cooking. Everything I had from the liquor cabinet, and especially my secret stash. It all had to go. I knew I had to avoid temptation. Have you done that yet, Mike?"

Mike was silent too long, which gave away his answer. Also,

Patricia recalled when he showed up at the church, Mike had commented that it was either that or go home and start drinking, which doubly confirmed her suspicions. He did have liquor still in the house. Patricia poked him in the ribs with her index finger. "He's going to do that tonight, aren't you, Mike?"

"I. . .but. . ."

"Aren't you, Mike?" she asked again.

Mike cleared his throat and stiffened in his chair. "Yes. Of course."

Having received the answer she needed, she turned back to Claude. "And what else helped you as you straightened yourself out?" She wanted to ask him exactly when he turned his life over to Christ, but didn't want to further intimidate Mike, who was being uncharacteristically quiet and pensive.

"After I got rid of all the booze, I joined a twelve-step group."

"What's that?"

"It's a twelve-week study on the twelve steps of AA. Every week the group discusses one step, and we all work at applying it to our lives."

Patricia nodded. "Bruce told me a little about that. He said they are all based on Biblical principles."

"Yes. I have quite a few Scripture references in my notes. I've already volunteered to lead the next program. I highly recommend that you do it, Mike. Actually, a few other new members are also interested. So if you want to do it, we can get a group started next week. But you can only do this if you're serious about turning your life around. It will only work for you when you're prepared to really apply yourself. Are you ready?"

Patricia turned to look at Mike. He sat silent in his chair, and his eyes flitted around the room, taking in the people who had shared their testimonies. His gaze stopped on one man in particular, and it was obvious he had been drinking before he arrived.

After a while, Mike cleared his throat. "Yes. I'm ready."

Claude stood, so Patricia stood also, and then Mike.

"Great," Claude said. "Give me your phone number, and I'll start arranging a time and meeting place, and I'll get back to you. If you'll excuse me, I have to go. I have a date with my wife tonight."

Claude grinned, and left.

৯৯

Mike sat in silence the entire drive home, staring out the window.

There had been a man, drunk, at the meeting. He'd never seen anything more pathetic in his life. Going drunk to an AA meeting was like. . .swearing in church or something. It wasn't right.

When he was on his way home after getting fired, it had almost been like a voice telling him to go see Patty. He'd listened because he knew if he didn't, he was going to start drinking the minute he arrived home. It wouldn't have been long after that, considering the state of mind he was in, he would soon have been too drunk to even stand. And then, knowing his luck lately, Patty would have shown up and dragged him to a meeting, and he wouldn't have fought her.

He would have been just like that drunk at an AA meeting. Pathetic. A loser.

When his father told him that his services were no longer required, the only thing on his mind was going home and drinking himself into oblivion. It had been the first and foremost thing on his mind, until he somehow got the idea in his head that seeing Patty was important. He tried to figure out when getting the next drink had become the most important thing in his life.

He couldn't.

He really was an alcoholic.

They stopped in front of his house, so he pushed the car door open and turned around. "Thanks for the ride, Patty, I. . .

Where are you going?"

She exited the car and closed the door behind her, so Mike did the same.

"We're going to dump all the booze in your house."

"We?"

"Yup."

Mike didn't move from beside the car, but Patty walked to his front door and waited.

He couldn't remember ever meeting someone so pushy. Only this time, they were on his turf, not hers. He was supposed to be the one giving the orders.

She crossed her arms and tapped her foot. "Are you coming or not?"

He shrugged his shoulders and started walking. He felt numb from his new revelation and probably needed someone to point him in the right direction for a little while, and Patty seemed just the right person to do it. Not wanting to look like he was giving in too easily, he squared his shoulders and forced himself to grin. "Do I have a choice?"

She shook her head. "Nope."

He unlocked the door and punched in the code for his alarm, then hung her jacket in the closet. "Welcome to my humble home."

She scanned the entranceway, noting the marble tile, ran her hand over the carved wood on the door, then tilted her head as she looked up the spiral staircase leading to the loft. "Nice place."

"Thanks." The house was clean and tidy, but that was only because the housekeeper had been there today. Since he no longer had a job, it looked like he would have to clean up his own mess for a while.

"We might as well get right to it. Where do you keep everything?"

He led her downstairs to the rec room. First her eyes widened at the sight of his home-theater television, then she turned her attention to the recessed bar, taking in the colored lights reflecting in the mirrors behind, and then the tooled wood of the bar unit itself, which was the focal point of the room. He'd built the bar with his friends and had spared no expense, including the mahogany top and custom-built leather stools.

Without saying a word, Patty gathered all the bottles on display and started pouring everything down the sink. She didn't miss a beat, pouring all the contents of every bottle without first reading the labels, nor did she check how much was actually in the bottles before she started pouring. One bottle's seal hadn't even been broken. Without hesitation, she cracked the seal and dumped it, too.

Mike tried not cringe when she picked up his bottle of the most expensive whiskey money could buy and poured the golden liquid down the sink with the rest. Next she opened the bottom shelves and dumped out everything else she could find.

The strong smell of sweet liquor permeated the air. Strangely, it turned his stomach.

He stared at his bottles lined up on the bar top. He counted an even dozen empty bottles. His mind went blank. It was all gone, every last drop. A woman he barely knew had just poured hundreds of his dollars down the drain.

She ran the water to complete the process. "Where's the rest?"

He spoke before he realized what he was saying. "In the linen closet."

"And the linen closet is. . .?"

Mike shook his head. He couldn't believe he'd told her, but he recognized that it was for his own good. He walked upstairs in a daze, straight to the linen closet where he reached behind the pile of towels and pulled out his secret last bottle.

Fortunately, she didn't question why he kept a bottle hidden when he lived alone. He wasn't sure he knew the answer.

Without a word, she marched into the kitchen and dumped it down the sink. "I'll take everything home and put them in my recycling bin for pickup, so you won't have to handle them again. Got a couple of bags?"

Woodenly, he found a few empty grocery bags and followed her as she returned downstairs to the rec room and watched as she put the bottles, one by one, into the bags.

The sound of clinking glass cruelly nagged at him as she picked everything up, reminding him what had just happened.

It was gone. Everything was gone.

He couldn't keep the sarcastic edge out of his voice, and he didn't care. "You enjoyed that, didn't you?"

She sighed. "No, I really didn't. It was such a waste. But Claude was right. It's for the best."

Mike bowed his head and pinched the bridge of his nose with his thumb and index finger. "I'm sorry. I didn't mean that. I know you're only doing what you think you have to do. And you're probably right."

The glass in the bags she was holding clinked again as Patty moved. "I think it's time for me to go."

Something in his chest tightened, gripping his heart like a vice. It was too early for him to be home alone. Nothing was on television. He didn't have anything to do. Just the thought of her leaving sent a stab of dread through him.

He rammed his hands into his pockets, but he couldn't keep still. He shuffled his feet, then stared at the empty shelves behind the bar.

This was it. He really had no choice. He was completely cut off; he had nothing unless he walked or called a cab to go to the closest bar for a case of beer, since by now all the liquor stores were closed. He could call one of his friends to bring him something if any of them were home and not already at the club. But he didn't want to drink. He couldn't. And he didn't want to see his friends, because by now they would all have consumed their share of alcohol. He would be the only one not drinking.

"Please. Stay."

"Stay? But. . ."

He opened his mouth to speak, but nothing came out. He didn't have any right to further inconvenience her. For the past three evenings, he'd kept her from her normal routine and her own friends, friends who were no doubt upright and respectable, friends who would never walk on the wrong side of the law, friends who probably didn't drink anything stronger than tea and liked it that way.

He wondered what her friends were like. He knew that she'd been raised going to church, then after graduating from high school, she'd attended Bible college, and right after that, she'd gone to work for her church. He suspected that everyone she knew, both friends and family, were Christians like her.

Mike had only ever known one person who was a Christian. Robbie was different from anyone he'd ever met, so different that for awhile he thought he'd been in love. He'd even asked her to marry him. For awhile he attended church with her, but even though he believed in God, religion wasn't for him. For awhile he'd managed to get her to pull away from church, hoping that he could make her lose interest in it altogether. In the end, she hadn't, and his interest strayed to someone he thought was more his type, someone who definitely didn't go to church. That hadn't worked out, either. Since then he'd dated a lot, but as soon as a woman looked like she was getting too serious, he ended it.

Of course, frequently women only went after him for his money, but he expected that. It went with the territory, and he treated them accordingly. Whenever he broke up with a woman, there weren't usually hard feelings, and life went on. It was all for fun, usually on both sides. So far, all his relationships had been shallow, and he hadn't been drawn to any woman in particular.

Until Patty. She was special. He liked her. She was tough

and confident, but at the same time, sweet and innocent. And she lived what she believed—standing up for what was right according to her God, no matter what. She had convictions. Strength. But at the same time, she was every inch a woman, tender and delicate. For the first time in a long time, he felt drawn to her by something he couldn't name, but it wasn't right. The woman was pure and wholesome, raised in a sheltered environment, and she chose to keep living that way.

He was none of the above. He'd been a wild and spoiled teenager, and he hadn't settled down much as an adult. He did what he wanted, when he wanted, the way he wanted. He lived to excess. But now, everything he'd done had caught up with him in one way or another. He'd broken the law and finally been caught. Because of his carelessness and disregard for the law or safety, someone had been hurt. Up until recently, he hadn't cared about anybody but himself.

Worst of all, there was no way to hide the severity of what he'd become from Patty, because she was his probation officer's sister. What she didn't already know, he had a feeling she would soon find out.

Then she'd hate him, and he'd deserve it.

Patty checked her watch. "All right," she said. "I'll stay, but not too long. I have a ladies' breakfast in the morning."

# four

Patricia wasn't sure if she was doing the smartest thing by staying, but she didn't know what else to do. She couldn't tell what was going on in his head, but something was happening in there, and she didn't think it was a good idea to leave him alone.

Mike smiled weakly. "Can I get you something to drink? I might have some tea or something here somewhere. I've got lots of pop in the fridge."

"Thanks for asking, but I'll pass."

She followed him upstairs into the living room where he flipped on the television, a newer, large-screen model, and sat in the center of a giant, well-stuffed couch. The room was well decorated in tones of blues. Everything was color coordinated, including a framed painting of a horse in a ranch scene hanging above a black gas fireplace, accented with polished brass. It was definitely masculine, yet comfortable.

Patricia sat in the armchair across from him. "You have a lovely home." She couldn't understand, though, why anyone living alone would need two televisions.

"Thank you." He laughed quietly. "I have to tell you, I seldom use the living room. When my friends come over, we usually head straight downstairs into the rec room, after everyone raids the kitchen."

She didn't know whether she should feel honored for the special treatment or bad for him, since it was also possible the only reason they were in the living room was that he felt too awkward about going down to the rec room after watching her dispose of his liquor. Over the years, she'd known a few people who had quit smoking, and a part of the addiction was

43

the breaking of bad habits and lifestyle patterns. She could only imagine that quitting drinking would have many similarities.

"So after you have your breakfast with the ladies tomorrow morning, what are you going to do?"

"I'm going out shopping with a friend. What are you doing tomorrow?"

"I have no idea, but I guess I'll think of something. Maybe I'll head to the shop and see how they're coming on my car."

As the hour passed, they watched a sitcom on the television in comfortable silence. At the end of the show, Mike politely thanked her for staying. She gathered up the bags of empty bottles and went home.

❧

Patricia settled into the passenger seat of Colleen's car, pushed her back into the chair, stretched her aching legs, wiggled her toes, and groaned. "I can't remember the last time I've done so much walking. My feet are killing me!"

"But it was worth it! Look at all the great stuff we bought."

"You mean the great stuff *you* bought. I only bought a new soap dispenser for the church."

"But it's a great soap dispenser." Colleen started the car. "I think your purse is ringing."

A muffled ring sounded. "Oh. It's probably Mom wanting to know if I'll be around for lunch after church tomorrow."

As quickly as she could, she dug under Colleen's parcels for her purse and pulled out her cellular phone. "Hello?"

"Hi, Patty. It's me. Mike. Did I catch you at a bad time?"

Patricia gasped and put her hand over the phone. "It's not my mom," she whispered to Colleen. "Excuse me. This might be private."

Colleen turned off the ignition, and Patricia stepped out of the car and closed the door. "Hi, Mike. Is something wrong?"

"No, nothing's wrong. I was just wondering if you could do me a favor. I hate to ask, but none of my friends are available.

My car is ready, and they don't want to leave it here outside over the weekend. I, uh, was wondering if you could come here and drive it home for me. I'll pay for a cab for you to get here. It's at Arnie's Auto Repair on Main Street."

Patricia checked her watch then glanced over at Colleen. "Actually, my friend was just about to drive me home. She can drop me off there instead."

"Thanks, I appreciate it. See you whenever you get here. I owe you."

Patricia turned off the phone and got back into Colleen's car. "Change of plans. I need you to drive me somewhere. I have to do a favor for a friend."

"A male or female friend?"

"None of your business."

"Ah. That kind of friend."

Patricia stared out the window. Colleen could think what she wanted. Maybe it would be safer for Mike if people thought she was dating him. She would suffer with the well-meaning but erroneous impressions of her love life, which was always a curiosity item around the church circles, but it would lessen the questions. Most of all, she wouldn't betray the confidence of Mike's personal life and the real reason they were together.

Come to think of it, she'd only meant to take him to one meeting. Since the day she met him, she'd seen him every day.

"Going to give me more details? What's he like? Where did you meet him? Does he go to our church? Do I know him?"

Patricia put on her best smile. "Shut up and drive me to Arnie's Auto Repair on Main."

Colleen smiled right back. "I can take a hint."

The entire way to Arnie's, Patricia gritted her teeth, listening to Colleen humming "Here Comes the Bride."

❧

Mike tossed his keys into the air, and once again stuffed them into his pocket while he waited alone, outside, beside his car.

His car was fixed, and it was killing him not to drive it. It was the stupidest thing. If he needed a ride, he could simply have called a cab, or, if he really wanted to start thinking of saving money while he was unemployed, he could take the bus.

It wasn't so simple when he needed someone else to drive his car. For a brief few seconds, he'd considered driving it home himself without a license. After all, he'd been cold sober for four days, and he was certainly a good driver. Unless he got a ticket or, heaven forbid, got in an accident, no one would ever know.

Except Patty. As soon as she knew his car was home, she would be bound to ask about it, and he knew he couldn't lie to her. He didn't want to disappoint her, and suddenly it mattered more than ever that he obeyed the restrictions of the charges against him. He got himself into this mess; it was nothing he didn't deserve, and he was going to get out of it the right way, with dignity.

Once again, he needed Patty. The only friend he'd been able to get in touch with was Wayne. However, he could tell that Wayne had been drinking. Therefore, he didn't want Wayne to drive his car.

How quickly things changed.

A red compact pulled into the lot. Patty exited and waved, but instead of the car immediately leaving, the woman who was driving hesitated and gave him an obvious going over. Any other time, he would have smiled, waved, and winked, openly flirting with any woman who paid him attention.

This time, he didn't feel like it. He smiled only at Patty as she started walking toward him, and the little red car drove away.

"Hi," he said as she approached. He couldn't keep his feet still. He left the side of his car, walked up to her, then took the bag she was carrying from her hand and walked side by side with her back toward his car. "I really appreciate this. And to show you how much, I want to take you out for dinner."

She shook her head. "Don't be silly. This is nothing."

They stopped beside his car. Before he realized what he was doing, he lifted his free hand and gently ran his fingertips along her soft cheek, slowly brushing away a stray lock of her beautiful brown hair. He didn't drop his hand, touching her chin as he spoke. "It isn't *nothing* to me, and I know what you're thinking. Yes, I can afford to take you out to dinner. I'm not quite derelict yet. I can easily get another job. I may have charges pending against me, but that doesn't make me unemployable. You deserve a special thank you."

She didn't fight his touch but stared up at him. It was the first time she'd stood so close to him, allowing him to assess her in a different way.

Their height difference was just about perfect. He didn't look down to see what kind of shoes she wore, but at the moment he was about five or six inches taller than she. To his way of thinking, that was just right for kissing. He knew she was about thirty, but with her sheltered lifestyle in mind, he wondered if she'd ever been kissed properly. He hoped not, because he wanted to be the one to do it.

She shivered slightly in the cool spring breeze then backed up one step, forcing him to drop his hand. "This is your car?"

He quirked up one side of his mouth in a lopsided smile. "Yeah." Patty had such beautiful eyes. He'd noticed the blue of her eyes when they had dinner together, but he hadn't been close enough to fully appreciate them. He'd never seen eyes such a pure blue without the aid of colored contacts, but she wasn't wearing any. That beautiful sky-blue was natural, and especially striking with her brown hair. He'd only ever seen the lighter blue eyes with blonds.

"You never told me your car would be like this. What is it? It's really expensive, isn't it? And I'll bet it's brand-new."

"Yeah, it's a limited edition, and it is fairly new." Unlike the other times they'd been together, today she wore a touch of eye shadow but no lipstick, although he suspected it had simply worn off. He found it almost funny that she'd worn makeup to go out with other women for breakfast but she didn't wear it for him. He'd always thought it was the other way around, at least it had been for most of the women he'd known.

He watched as she stared at his car in wide-eyed fascination then ran her hand cautiously over the hood of the low-slung sports coupe. "And you trust me to drive this?"

He trusted her with more than just his car; he trusted her with his life. "Of course I trust you, or I wouldn't have asked. And I also trust that you won't argue with me, and you'll drive it to where I say I want to go."

"I've been shopping all day. I really don't feel like going someplace fancy. Besides, I'm not dressed for it."

"Then where we're going will be perfect." He opened the driver's door and bowed with a flourish. Her mouth opened then snapped shut, and she begrudgingly got in.

After he gave her directions and they were on their way, he selected a CD, turned it to a low volume, and settled back in the seat. He'd thought he would feel awkward being a passenger in his own car. Normally, he didn't like being a passenger in anyone's car. The first time Patty picked him up, he felt strange, but the second time, he'd been relaxed. Now, in his own car, he didn't mind her driving at all.

"How did you get my cell number?"

"I phoned your place, but when I got the answering machine, I called the church, in case you were there. I ended up speaking to the pastor. He wasn't going to give me your number, but when I gave him my name, he must have remembered what a good job I did sorting those paper clips, because he gave it to me without hesitation after that."

Her lips tightened, but he noticed she didn't say anything. Now more than before, he considered it a mark in his favor to have obtained her cell number so easily.

She pulled into the parking lot. Mike couldn't help but smile when she parked in a spot far away from the rest of the other cars. He always did the same thing to preserve the pristine paint on his car's doors for as long as he could.

She handed him the keys, and he pushed the button for the alarm.

"I can see why you alarm your house, but your car?"

"It's better to be safe than sorry."

He guided her up the steps and escorted her inside his favorite bistro where a table was waiting despite the lineup.

"You made a reservation?"

He shrugged his shoulders and patted the cell phone hanging on his belt. "They know me here."

Unlike the last time they had dinner together, Mike didn't complain about a single thing, even in jest. This time, he didn't have the pressure of going to an AA meeting hanging over his head. Also, he wanted to make it up to Patty for being so difficult the last time they were together, because he usually wasn't so hard to get along with, nor did he usually complain so much. His behavior embarrassed him, and he wanted to make it right.

When the waiter asked what they wanted to drink before he took their order for their meals, his usual drink order nearly slipped out of his mouth before he thought about it, it had become so ingrained in his routine. Patty ordered coffee, and before he had a chance to speak, asked him in front of the waiter if he wanted a coffee as well, sparing him the awkward moment.

The warm coffee didn't feel right, so he pushed it aside and concentrated on entertaining Patty. Today she was there as his date, and he treated her as such.

When their meals came, he hesitated when Patty stopped to pray before they ate. This time was different than when they were at Sir Henry's, because the restaurant was crowded. However, either because of the crowd, or out of consideration for him, she made her prayer quick and to the point, and it was over so fast he barely noticed.

He had to admire her. It was important to her to say grace before each meal, even in public, and she was sticking to that. She had not backed down even though she knew he really didn't want to pray. Despite the possibility of his protests, she had done what she considered the right thing, which was to thank God for the meal, not caring that people might stare at them in a public place.

As the evening progressed, it wasn't difficult to make Patty smile. It was important to him that she enjoy herself, and it was easy to get her to do. Her face was an open book. In the same way he could tell when she was annoyed with him or nervous in an unfamiliar situation, he could also see that she was enjoying herself, and he was encouraged. He very carefully steered the conversation away from his troubles and away from anything that might be considered business or to do with church, and simply had a good time.

Mike was extremely pleased with himself when she didn't argue with him about the bill, which was the smallest he could remember, because there was no alcohol consumed with the meal.

He left his credit card on the tray with the bill and turned to Patty while the waiter completed the transaction. "You're certainly a cheap date. We're going to have to do this more often."

Instead of an answer, Patty held her palm to her mouth and yawned, and then her face turned red. "I'm so sorry! I'm really tired after running around all day, and all this good food is putting me to sleep. I have to get up early for church in the morning. We should be going."

Her response didn't do wonders for his ego, but Mike chose to conclude that since she didn't have a negative response, that they would indeed do this again.

When she pulled his car into the driveway, instead of turning it off, she started searching under the seat and behind the visor.

"What are you doing?" he asked.

"I'm looking for your garage door opener. I assume you're going to want to keep your car in the garage rather than the driveway for the next few months."

He hadn't really thought about it. "Actually, the battery was dead, so it's in the house. I'm sure the limits of not driving don't include moving the car from the driveway into the garage. After all, it's on my own property. Don't worry about it."

They both exited the car, and Mike waited for Patty to come around to his side.

"Can I use your phone book?" she asked.

"Sure. What for?"

"I have to call a cab so I can go home."

Mike stopped in his tracks, and Patty also stopped walking.

"No. Don't do that." He glanced at his car then back to Patty. "Take my car."

"Take your car? But. . ." Her voice trailed off. "I can't do that."

"Why not? I'm obviously not going to be using it."

"You trust me with your car?"

"You're a good driver. Take it."

"I can't."

"I already said you can. You've got to get home."

She looked back and forth between him and the car. "How do you know I won't abuse it, or drive carelessly, or sell it and take off with the money or something?"

Mike laughed. "Just by saying those things, you've proved that you wouldn't."

"But you barely know me."

His mouth opened, but no words came out. It was true; he didn't know her all that well in some ways, but in others, he knew her better than she thought. Dozens of Patty's finer qualities ran through his head as he considered what he could tell her that he already knew about her.

She was kind, yet firm. She'd gone out of her way to be helpful, but at the same time knew where to draw the line. He thought she had a great sense of humor, although at times she bordered on sarcasm, but her sharp wit only proved her intelligence. Her sense of right and wrong was as solid as black and white. He even admired her for her unwavering Christianity, which, by itself, said a lot about her. She was a good leader, although she tended to be bossy, but by being so, she also displayed confidence and a great strength of character, which she would need. After all, he knew how headstrong he could be, and that was what she was up against.

He liked her, and he liked her a lot. He couldn't think of a single thing to say that wouldn't sound sappy, so he stuck with "I trust you."

Instead of the fast comeback he expected, she stood before him with her mouth hanging open. Her confusion only magnified her sweetness.

He wanted to kiss her.

"Well, I guess I should go home. Good night, Mike." She jingled his keys in her hand.

Before she turned around, Mike glanced at his car, then back to Patty. "This is so backwards. I'm supposed to be the one to say good night and drive away."

She shrugged her shoulders. "Life seldom goes the way we think it will."

Mike stepped closer. "Thanks for picking up my car. More than that, I really enjoyed being with you tonight." He'd enjoyed himself more than he had in a long time. They'd discussed nothing important, only relaxed in each other's company, enjoying the moment exactly as it was—simply spending time together. He wondered if this was what it was like to really fall in love.

Patty smiled, sending a warmth through his heart. "Yes, it was nice."

He was hoping for a better summary than *nice,* but Mike decided to take what he could get. "May I kiss you good night?"

"Sure."

Before he could move closer to embrace her and kiss her properly, she turned her head all the way to the side, tilted up her chin, and tapped her index finger to her cheek.

Mike smiled. If she wanted to play games, that was fine with him. He was good at playing games.

Instead of a quick peck on the cheek, he nuzzled his face into her hair, inhaled the apple fragrance of her shampoo, and smiled as he nibbled and kissed her ear. Very slowly and gently, he rested his hands on her shoulders, and moved his mouth to her cheek, brushing gentle kisses closer and slower as he worked his way to her mouth. Gently, he brushed the underside of her chin with one finger, then two, until he was ready to turn her face toward his and kiss her fully.

Just as he was about to claim her mouth, she stepped back, breaking contact except for one hand remaining on her shoulder, preventing him from doing what he wanted.

"Watch it. I know karate. I took a women's self-defense course. Of course, I could always call my brother on his cell phone and tell him to come and beat you up."

Mike let his hand drop from her shoulder. "Beat me up? But. . ." He couldn't imagine anyone asking such a thing of a probation officer, whose job held very rigid restrictions against violence and using unnecessary force. Unless she was speaking of Bruce in the capacity of a big brother, protecting his little sister from unwanted advances. "Not funny," he muttered.

"I didn't mean it to be funny. Good night, Mike."

Mike watched the taillights of his car disappear in the distance. Patty Norbert won this round, but he'd win the next.

# five

Patricia sighed as she hung up the phone. In the back of her mind, she had hoped that Mike would have shown up at church yesterday, but he hadn't. She didn't want to miss him, but she did.

She buried her face in her hands. She'd almost melted in his arms the last time they'd been together. She thought she was being so smart, offering only her cheek when she knew he wanted more, but he had quickly turned that situation to his favor. She'd given him an inch, and he'd taken a mile. The trouble was, his actions had heightened all her senses, and for the moment, she did want him to kiss her.

She wished she knew what had been going through Mike's head when he tried that. It seemed that her inexperience with men was inversely proportional to his experience with women.

Michael Flannigan, Jr., was dangerous.

If it was anyone else, she would simply refuse to see him again, and that would be the end of it. But she couldn't. She had his car.

She had underestimated him.

It would never happen again.

The phone rang again, bringing her attention back to where it should have been in the first place, away from Mike and back to her job, which was the administration of serving God's people.

After successfully dealing with a parent who insisted that her child was too developed for the toddler class, and kept insisting the three year old be moved into the grade one class, Patricia needed a break.

Today was a day that demanded an early lunch break.

Nothing would soothe her nerves more than the friendly little squirrel at the park bench, who hopefully had missed her handouts all weekend.

Patricia gathered a few slices of bread along with her sandwich and went outside.

Sure enough, the little brown squirrel appeared not long after she sat down. Just like every day, she leaned over, holding a small piece of bread gently in her fingers, encouraging the little creature to take it from her hand. When he finally approached and took it, Patricia slowly sat back on the bench, picked another morsel of bread out of the bag, and waited for it to finish the treat, all ready to give it the next one.

"Hi, Patty. Mind if I join you?"

Patricia screeched, and the bread flew out of her fingers. The squirrel fled.

"Oops. Did I startle you? Sorry."

Patricia pressed her palm to her pounding heart. "Mike! What are you doing here?"

He shuffled beside her on the bench. "I was just in the neighborhood and thought I'd stop by. It wasn't like I had anything better to do."

She wasn't sure if she was supposed to feel complimented, so she said nothing.

"Cute little chipmunk. I guess I scared it away."

"It's a squirrel. Chipmunks have a stripe down their backs, and their tails are short. A squirrel has a long bushy tail, and they come in all colors."

"I knew that." He grinned. "I was just teasing you. Can I feed him with you?"

"I'm not sure he'll come back, but if he does, you're welcome to try. He's still really shy about taking the bread out of my hand, but we're working on it."

They both sat back on the bench, talking quietly about nothing in particular while they waited for the squirrel to return. After awhile, it didn't, so Mike leaned back, crossed his ankles, clasped his hands together over his stomach, and generally made himself comfortable. The breeze ruffled his hair, and he closed his eyes and sighed contentedly. Just looking at him made her think how much he must have needed this stress break. It was the same reason why she enjoyed taking her lunch outside with the squirrel.

"How did you get here?" she asked.

He didn't open his eyes. "I rode my bike. For two reasons. First, I cashed in my membership at the gym to save money, then I thought I'd get some exercise. And I missed you." He opened one eye and smiled. Patricia's breath caught. "I guess that's really three reasons, and they weren't in the right order."

She didn't want him to miss her.

"I see my car in the parking lot. I'm glad you're using it."

"Uh. . .yes. . ." She felt her cheeks heat up. It was a rare treat to drive such a car, because she would never be able to afford such a machine, even if she ever had an inclination to own a car like that. She also wanted to drive it when no one she knew would see her with it, so she figured that taking it to work and back on Monday would get it out of her system.

"Claude called me this morning. He said that special group is starting tonight, and we'll be meeting at his house. I called Bruce, and he's going to come with me to the first few meetings. So I won't be able to see you tonight."

Patricia wondered why he was telling her this, because even if she had plans for the evening, they wouldn't have been with Mike. But still, part of her wanted to know what he was doing, strictly because she was concerned for him as one of Bruce's cases, of course.

He checked his watch. "I think your lunch break is over, it's time for you to get back inside. I'll phone you or something."

To Patricia's shock, he simply stood and walked away. As she gathered up her lunch containers, out of the corner of her eye, she watched him mount a mountain bike that had been

*My Name Is Mike* 57

set near the side wall and ride off.

Patricia sighed as she sat down at her desk and pulled out the notes her father had made from the budget meeting. It was going to be a long day.

※

Patricia leaned forward on the park bench, her hand outstretched. Just as the day before, the little brown squirrel approached slowly. She loved it when it took the bread from her fingers, and now she would have to handle the little creature with patience, until the day it wouldn't run too far away to eat the treats she gave it. One day, she hoped she would be able to take a picture of it from close range while it was eating.

When it was mere inches away, it froze.

"Hi, Patty. Mind if I join you?"

The squirrel darted away at the same time as she screeched, and the bread once again flew from her fingers.

She leaned her elbows on her knees and buried her face in her hands. "Hi, Mike."

"Are you trying to feed that chipmunk again? Do you feed that thing every day?"

"It's a squirrel, and yes, I do feed it every day. I've been working very hard to get it to take the bread from my fingers."

"Oops. Sorry."

She straightened and took a sip of her juice as he slid beside her on the bench. "How did the meeting go yesterday?"

His whole body stiffened. "I don't know how to describe it. At first, it was a kind of a get-to-know-you kind of thing. Like, by the end of this thing we're supposed to be pouring our guts out to each other, so we can't be total strangers. Claude opened with a prayer, which was okay, I guess, and then we went over AA's first step, which is 'We admitted we were powerless over alcohol—that our lives had become unmanageable.' It was so strange. We could all relate to each other, and we all could admit that. But it was different to actually say it out loud. Know what I mean?"

Patricia nodded. "Confession is good for the soul. There is tremendous value in verbalizing your feelings to solidify your position in a difficult situation."

He blinked, and stared at her. "Okay. . . ."

Her cheeks burned. She hadn't meant to turn into counselor mode. That was Bruce and Claude's responsibility. "Sorry. I sometimes get carried away. There's an old saying that confession is good for the soul."

"What was really different was praying about it. Thinking about it is one thing. Telling someone else is another. But to close my eyes and talk to God about it, well, it's something I've never done before."

She laid one hand on his forearm as she spoke. "You can talk to God about anything, Mike. And the best part is, He's always there to listen."

"I guess. Hey! Look. Your chipmunk is back."

Very slowly, Patricia bent at the waist and held out the piece of bread. The little squirrel took the morsel and scampered a safe distance away. They sat in silence watching it eat. When the critter was done, instead of approaching for more, it scampered off into the bush.

"So, what are you doing tonight?"

"This is Tuesday. Every Tuesday I go to a Bible study meeting. Want to come?" She forced herself to smile, but inside, her heart pounded, and she nearly broke out into a cold sweat. She wanted him to come. She would have preferred to talk to him about God one-on-one, but she also knew that he would benefit from a group situation with other believers. Mike believed in God, but at the time, he had been more than a little sarcastic as she told him about God's love for His children. She didn't know how much he participated in the prayer, but he did say he talked to God, which was encouraging.

"I don't think so. I'm not really into that kind of thing."

She tried to hide her disappointment but knew she wasn't

doing a very good job when he leaned forward and grasped her hands within his. "Is it important to you that I go?"

Patricia didn't know what to say. It was important. She wanted him to have a right relationship with God, but she didn't want him to begin his journey of discovery because of her. He had to do it for himself. "No, not really."

Silence hung in the air for a short time. She was about to ask about arranging to return his car when he started talking about nothing in particular, making pleasant small talk. Patricia enjoyed talking to him so much that she didn't realize the passage of time until Mike checked his watch, announced that it was time for her to get back to work, and left.

He walked away before she realized she had missed the chance to ask him about the car. She wondered if he did it on purpose.

≥≥

Patricia hit Save and tidied her stack of papers before she went into the kitchen to get her lunch as well as a couple of pieces of bread that she stored there for the little squirrel.

As she sat on the bench to eat, she thought about last night's Bible study meeting, part of her regretting that she hadn't been more direct with Mike and specifically requested that he come, and part of her being glad he hadn't been there.

They had covered the story of Jonah, focusing on how much Jonah would have suffered in the belly of the fish. And that, although it was often hard work to follow God's will, it would have been easier on Jonah if he'd just done what he had been told to do in the first place. Their discussion naturally followed to a more personal level, and a number of the people present shared recent experiences where they felt led to do something out of the ordinary for God and told about how they'd handled it.

She hadn't shared about Mike because she didn't want to risk breaking confidentiality, but the lesson further solidified in her own mind what she was called to do, which was to guide Mike through this trying time and help him build a relationship with Jesus as his Savior.

A movement on a nearby tree caught her eye. Quickly, she returned the uneaten part of her sandwich to the container, ripped off a small piece of bread from her special stash for the squirrel, slowly leaned over, and held it out. The little brown squirrel approached cautiously, then in the blink of an eye snatched the bread from her fingers and ran into the bush.

"Hi, Mike," she called over her shoulder without looking as the squirrel retreated out of sight.

The grass rustled behind her. "How did you know I was coming? I scared your chipmunk again, didn't I?"

"It's a squirrel."

He grinned as he shuffled in beside her. This time he carried a small backpack. He withdrew a sandwich, grinned, and placed it on the bench. "It's not exactly going out for dinner together, but I brought dessert." He removed a couple of store-bought pieces of cake, also nicely wrapped, and put them down with the growing lunch pile.

"Uh. . .thank you."

He unwrapped his sandwich and took a bite, so Patricia also took a bite of hers.

"There is a reason for this, you know."

"There is?" Patricia couldn't remember anything special about the day.

"It's the anniversary of our first meeting. Kind of like the celebration of our first date."

She nearly choked on her sandwich. "First date? We haven't had a first date."

"That's not my fault. So are we on for tonight?"

All she could do was stare at him. After she got home from the Bible study meeting, she'd spent many hours in prayer, agonizing over what to do and thinking how she could show Mike how much God loved him. She had to make him see God as more than simply the Supreme Creator, but also his

Heavenly Father, Who sent His Son, Jesus, to take the punishment for his sins.

As a ministry, she could make no allowances for dating, even if he was her type, which he wasn't. Most importantly, she couldn't risk becoming emotionally involved, because it would jeopardize her mission.

Patricia cleared her throat. "No."

He shrugged his shoulders, but didn't lose the grin. "Oh, well. I had to try. Bruce is taking me to another meeting tonight anyway. I'm not sure I'll see you tomorrow. I've got an interview for a job, and I don't know what time I'll be finished."

"Mike! That's great!"

Before she realized what she was doing, she looked down to see that she had wrapped her fingers around his.

She jerked her hands away, then folded them in her lap. "I have to get back inside soon. We should finish up."

He had the nerve to wink as he bit into his sandwich.

&

Mike sat on the bus, staring out the window. He wanted to hit something.

Hard.

The interview had gone smoothly, until he told them he would need a day or two off in a couple of months when his court case came up. He knew he would probably get off, or if he did get anything, it probably would only be a fine and a suspended license for a while. At the worst, he might have to spend a few weekends in jail. His father had hired one of the best lawyers in town to defend him. That, plus showing the judge that he was being such a good boy by attending AA meetings without protest, according to the terms laid out for him, plus that it was a first offense, all would act in his favor.

He didn't get the job. Because he was honest about his pending court case, they suddenly became uninterested. If he had said nothing and just taken a couple of days off sick when his court date came up, no one would have known.

They didn't hire him because of that.

And for that, he'd missed having lunch with Patty.

Already he missed her. He hadn't been without her for a day, and he missed her.

He stomped all the way from the bus stop into the house, his big empty house. He threw his jacket on the couch, stood in one spot, closed his eyes, and yelled out in frustration. It hadn't been exactly the job he would have chosen, but anything was better than sitting home alone in an empty house all day, every day.

Mike checked the time and laid his hand on the phone. He wanted to see Patty. If he couldn't see her, he had to talk to her.

He didn't dial. Instead, he thought about what was happening. He had never been so compelled to spend time with a woman. With the odd exception, by now, most women would have been eating out of his hand, and he would be enjoying himself immensely.

But Patty wasn't. He wasn't even sure she wanted to spend time with him at all.

Every time they were together, she seemed to enjoy herself, and she certainly seemed comfortable enough with him. Still, he could tell something was bugging her. It bothered him that she was his probation officer's sister, and it was probably a breech of confidence or crossing into forbidden territory to be seeing her, which meant it wasn't a good idea to get too attached to her.

He couldn't help it. She'd done nothing to encourage him, in fact, just the opposite. She'd refused to go out on a date with him, and she wouldn't let him kiss her properly. She never called him; he had always been the one to either call her or simply just show up when she couldn't get away.

Mike released the phone. He wasn't going to call her, and he wasn't going to show up on her doorstep.

For the first time in his life, he didn't know what to do.

Mike looked at the Bible she'd lent him, still lying on the kitchen counter where he'd left it since she'd given it to him a week ago. He had no idea on what page to start reading, so he didn't touch it.

Since he couldn't think of anything else to do, Mike walked into the living room and sat on the couch. He started to reach for the remote, but didn't pick it up. He didn't want to watch television. He had to think.

Any other day, he would be pouring himself a drink and nursing it while he thought about what was bothering him, until whatever it was faded in importance or his brain became so dulled he forgot what he was so worried about in the first place. This time he couldn't, because Patty had poured everything down the drain, which had been a good thing. If there had been anything left in the house, he would have been into it by now.

All he could do was stare at the blank television.

He wanted to phone Patty, to pursue a relationship with her, but he couldn't. She wasn't his type. She was a decent and caring person, putting her time and needs aside to do what was best for others. She deserved better than him. She deserved a man who would treat her right. Looking back on his past relationships, he'd never treated a woman right, and he'd been too self-centered to care.

She was also his probation officer's sister. Not only was he positive he was crossing some kind of line he wasn't supposed to, he wondered what Bruce would do when he found out that one of his alcoholic law-breaking cases had the hots for his sister.

Mike buried his face in his hands. To even think of Patty in such a way was insulting to her. What he felt for her was far beyond physical attraction. But whatever it was, it wasn't right. She was smart enough to know it and to try to keep him at a distance. It was because she was so nice that she wasn't doing a very good job of keeping him away.

On the other hand, Mike couldn't let it drop. She was too good to let go. He just didn't know what to do about it.

Therefore, he did the only thing he could. He folded his hands in his lap, closed his eyes, and for the first time in his life, he prayed to a God Whom, up until recently, he had ignored, and hoped that God would listen anyway.

# six

"Hi, Patty. Busy tonight?"

Silence hung over the line. Mike held his breath.

"Uh. . .no. . . ."

He forced himself to exhale. He hadn't seen her or talked to her in two days, and he was going crazy. "I was wondering, if you weren't busy, if we could go out for dinner, someplace quiet where we could talk and without the caveat of attending another AA meeting afterwards."

"Uh. . ." Her voice trailed off, and silence again hung over the line.

Mike waited. He wasn't going to beg. It wasn't his style.

"I don't know if that's such a good idea."

He flushed his style down the toilet. He needed results more than he needed to salvage his pride, which was already in tatters anyway. "Please? We'll have a nice time. I know we will, and I'll behave."

"Uh. . .well. . .I guess so."

He pulled one fist down in the air while making a closed-teeth triumphant smile and thinking "Yessss!" in his head. "That's wonderful," he said calmly. "The only catch here is that since you've got my car, you've got to pick me up. But I'll pay for the gas."

"Don't be silly. And about your car, I think it's time I gave it back."

"We can talk about it tonight. How's that?"

"I guess so."

"Great. Can you pick me up at six?"

"Sure. But remember, I have church tomorrow morning, so this can't be a late night."

"No problem. See you later."

Mike smiled as he hung up the phone. It was going to be the best Saturday night of his life.

By the time she arrived, Mike was composed and ready. He shaved for the second time that day and gelled his hairstyle to perfection. He chose a casual black shirt and his black jeans, knowing how sharp he looked in the monochrome ensemble, which would be suitable attire no matter where they went. He grabbed his favorite leather jacket, clipped his cell phone to his belt, and locked up as soon as his car pulled into the driveway.

He picked a suitable restaurant once he saw how she was dressed. Today she wore a loose-fitting jean skirt and a pretty pink pullover top. It pleased him to see that this time she'd applied a little bit of makeup, but her hair still hung loose, just the way he liked it.

The same as every time he joined her for lunch at the park bench, their evening together was pleasant. Since he knew before he asked her out for dinner that she would pray before they ate, he was prepared when she did. After she'd said the expected thank-you for the food and friends to share it with, he was very honest in his answering "amen," because he felt the same way.

When they were done, she drove him home, and he invited her in so he could ask a few questions.

First he made coffee, then sat beside her on the couch and opened the Bible she'd loaned him to the page he had marked.

"I cannot tell a lie. I didn't start reading where you told me to."

She raised one finger in the air and opened her mouth, but he raised his hand to stop her before she got the wrong idea and became disappointed with him.

"I flipped through and read all the verses you had colored in yellow. I figured if you thought they were important enough to mark up your Bible for, then that was what I should be paying the most attention to."

"That's not necessarily true. When I do highlighting, it's when I'm reading and something has a special meaning to me at the time. Those things aren't going to hit you the same way, especially since this is your first time reading it through."

"What do you mean, reading it through?"

"Reading it cover to cover. Although I had told you to first read the New Testament. I've read the Bible through four times now, four different versions. I have a guidebook that says how much to read in both the Old and New Testaments each day, and it gives a small commentary on those verses. The idea is to read the entire Bible through in one year. It's dated. You start January first, kind of like a New Year's resolution kind of thing, and finish up the same year on December thirty-first. But the very first time I read it, I simply started at Genesis 1:1 and read some every day until I got to Revelation 22:21. I think it took me about five months."

Mike stared at the Bible in his hand, then flipped through the pages. He didn't know much about the Bible, but he did know that Genesis was the first book and Revelation was the last. Not only was it really thick, but he found out the hard way that it wasn't like reading a best-selling novel. Some of the verses he had to reread four times in order to fully comprehend the meaning of a single sentence, and even then, he knew without a doubt that he'd still missed stuff. He couldn't imagine reading the whole thing through, especially different versions in which he knew the wording was slightly different. "Wow. . . ," he mumbled.

"Did you have something you were going to ask me?"

"Oops. I lost my place. It was something about Moses and Jesus."

She laughed. "There are more references to Moses and Jesus in the Bible than I could count. I guess you'll have to reread it and then ask me when you find it again."

He stared at the closed Bible. He'd taken hours paging through it and reading the verses she'd highlighted. However, it had been both interesting and thought-provoking, and he supposed it wouldn't hurt to go through it again. "I guess I don't have much choice."

"It really would be a better idea for you to start where I said, the beginning of the book of Matthew, and read it through. That way, you'll be reading everything in context, and it will be easier to understand."

Mike shrugged his shoulders. "I guess you would know."

Patty checked her watch. "I have to go. Remember, I have church in the morning. And you know you're invited if you want to come. It's not like you've never been there before." She smiled, and Mike's heart nearly went into overdrive.

"Yeah. I know," he choked out.

She stood. "Can I borrow your phone book? I have to call a cab."

Mike shook his head. "Forget the cab. Take the car. I'm not using it, and it's getting late. You'll wait a long time for a cab on Saturday night, and I'd feel better knowing you're in my car."

"I really shouldn't."

Mike stood as well and grasped her tiny hands in his. Her skin was so soft, and he didn't often have the chance to touch her. Very slowly and gently, he massaged the tender skin of her wrists with his thumbs, enthralled how such a simple action could move him so much. "You won't take my heart, so please take my car."

"I. . ." Her voice trailed off and the cutest blush colored her cheeks.

Mike smiled. "If you don't take the car and go now, I'm going to embarrass myself and start spouting poetry."

She yanked her hands out of his, walked quickly to the door, then nearly ran outside.

"Wait!" he called out, and ran to catch up to her, which he did as she opened the car door. He made sure to lower his voice so his neighbors couldn't overhear, in case anyone was outside. "I didn't get a good night kiss."

Before she had a chance to protest, he tilted her chin up and brushed a soft kiss quickly to her lips, then backed away.

She looked up at him, her eyes wide. His heart pounded, making him question why, because he really hadn't done anything all that exciting, although what passed between them was special in a way he couldn't name. It made him want to kiss her again, properly this time, but he didn't dare.

"Good night, Mike," she said in almost a whisper, then sank into the car and drove away.

Mike watched until she turned the corner, but he couldn't make his feet move.

He knew where he was going in the morning. Strangely, it wasn't entirely to be with Patty.

He couldn't remember the specifics of a single verse he'd read, but what he had read made him want to know more about the God Who created him. Was it possible that God really did love him as much as the verses he'd read had said?

❧

Patricia stood beside her mother as they greeted the earliest of the congregation to arrive and handed each person a bulletin. While her mother chatted with a friend, Bruce and his wife entered.

Bruce pulled a computer disk out of his pocket. "I brought that clip-art you were asking me about."

"Thanks! I really appreciate it. Let me go put it on my desk."

He followed her into the office. "I took Mike Flannigan to another AA meeting during the week. He told me that he'd been to another meeting with you, as well, before that one."

"Yes, that's right," she mumbled as she tucked the disk into the right file folder.

"I left a message on your answering machine last night, just to be sure I copied the right file for you, but you never called me back."

Patricia faltered for just a split second. "Sorry, I didn't get .

home until late. I must have forgotten to check for messages."

"Oooh," Bruce drawled, then leaned back on the filing cabinet. "Hot date?"

"Not really. I just went out to dinner with Mike."

Bruce froze. "Mike who?"

"Which Mike were we just talking about? Mike Flannigan."

"You went out on a date with him?"

"It wasn't a date. It was just dinner."

"Patty, going out to dinner with a man on a Saturday night *is* a date."

She muttered a denial under her breath but doubted he heard.

"Okay, I can see you don't want to talk about it. That's fine." He turned his head to gaze out the window and study the parking lot. "I was surprised to see you here this morning. I didn't see your car in the lot."

"I didn't bring my car."

"Is there something wrong with that hunk of junk again? Do you need a ride home?"

Patricia closed the desk drawer and walked toward the door, en route to the foyer. "I haven't made an appointment with the mechanic yet, but for now it's still driveable. Thanks for the offer, but I don't need a ride home. I brought Mike's car." At the beginning of the week, she didn't want anyone to see her driving it, but as time went on, she enjoyed it so much in comparison to her own car that she found herself not wanting to give it up. Besides, the use of it now had become very convenient, since her car needed a trip to the repair shop that she wanted to put off paying for.

Bruce quickly caught up with her, then stopped her about a foot out of the office doorway. "Mike's car? What are you doing with Mike's car?"

"I helped him pick it up after it was fixed, and the right moment hasn't come up to give it back."

"Right moment? How long have you had it?"

Patricia counted on her fingers. "Eight days."

Bruce sputtered and pulled her back into the office then shut the door behind them. "What's going on? Why has he given you his car? Do you know who he is?"

She blinked and stiffened her back. "He's just an ordinary guy who needs a little help to get his life on the right track."

"He's no ordinary guy. He has a history of drinking and I suspect some drug abuse even though this is the first time he's been officially charged. The fact is that I'm his probation officer for a reason. He's in big trouble, and I don't think he's taking it seriously. He's rich and spoiled and manipulative, and he eats innocent women like you for breakfast."

She crossed her arms and stared at her brother. "I think you're getting carried away."

"He's bad news, Patty. Stay away from him. I mean it."

Patricia narrowed her eyes. She couldn't believe the way Bruce was behaving. "Aren't you being rather judgmental?"

"I'm his probation officer. It's my job to be judgmental. And I'm his probation officer for a reason. This isn't just a parking ticket. He deserves the charges he's been given."

"Maybe so, but whom I see is not your concern."

"It is when you're wrong. He's not the kind of man you should be seeing. Most of all, he's not a Christian."

"You don't know that."

"Yes, I do. I've seen him in action under pressure. You didn't see him the night he was arrested. I had to go down to the police station in the middle of the night when his rich daddy posted bail. He's not only a drunk, he's an arrogant drunk. And I'm not convinced that his performance at AA meetings isn't just an act because he thinks that he can manipulate the justice system. He thinks if he shows the judge that he's reformed, he can get a lighter sentence. I've seen it before with his type."

She couldn't deny that Mike had a bit of an attitude, but she refused to listen to Bruce insult him any longer. She really believed that Mike was trying. He'd started reading her Bible, even if it wasn't the way she'd told him to do it. It also shocked her to hear of Bruce talk that way about anyone, especially Mike. She could understand how his experiences with people at his job would harden him to some degree, but she didn't want to think her brother could be so unforgiving and unwilling to give Mike a chance to redeem himself.

"I can't believe the way you're acting. Aren't you the one who pushed him into going to AA meetings so that he could straighten out?"

Bruce dragged his palm over his face. "I'm sorry. I'm not usually like this. You're my sister. I don't want to see you get mixed up with the likes of Mike Flannigan. I don't want him to take advantage of you or hurt you."

"So far, I'm the one taking advantage of him. Have you had a look at that car he's let me borrow without asking for a thing in return?"

"Don't think he won't. He'll ask for something in exchange when he knows you can't turn him down."

Mike's silly comment about taking his car versus his heart crashed to the front of her mind with a thud. She knew he was only teasing, but still, the remote possibility that he wasn't scared her. "I plan to give the car back as soon as I can, today if possible. But I don't want to hear you telling me who I can and cannot spend my time with. That's my business, not yours."

Bruce's face paled, and he backed up a step. "Sorry," he mumbled, and without further comment, he walked away.

Patricia felt sick. She'd just had a fight with her brother, whom she loved, over a man she barely knew.

What bothered her most of all was that Bruce was right. Mike wasn't her type. Mike was rich and spoiled, and he did have a bad attitude, and she could tell he was a ladies' man. Worst of all, she kind of liked him anyway, although she couldn't figure out why. If all that wasn't bad enough, even though she'd known all along that, according to all the rules, it wasn't a good idea for her to minister to him, God kept throwing Mike in her path.

Therefore, she would obey, and she would do what she could to guide Mike in a path to knowing Jesus Christ as his Savior, if that was what Mike chose to do.

She sucked in a deep breath, absently ran her hands down her sleeves to push out some imaginary creases, and returned to the foyer to chat with some friends who had just arrived.

⁂

Mike held himself straight and tall and walked into the church building. Even though it had been over three years ago, it wasn't like he'd never been to church before. He'd already been to this one a number of times, although it was during the week when it was quiet and business as usual, whatever that meant in a church. However, today it felt different with the buzz of people around him and music in the background.

It didn't take him long to find Patty. Her joyous laugh warmed him deep inside and drew him like a magnet.

He joined the small group she was with and stood beside her. He smiled, quickly nodded a greeting at everyone in the small circle, and moved closer to Patty when she noticed him. "Hi," he said, grinning ear-to-ear.

"Mike! What are you, uh, I mean, it's good to see you here."

He could feel the other women in the group staring at him, which happened often when he joined a conversation already in progress. This time, he didn't care to smile back at the other ladies. The only person whose attention he wanted was Patty's.

She looked beautiful. She wore a lovely spring-type dress in a soft flowing blue fabric and matching shoes. It was feminine and pretty, and it suited her.

"These are my friends, Colleen, Nancy, and Fran. And this is Mike."

He nodded at each as they were introduced. Nancy and Fran politely excused themselves and walked away together, peeking over their shoulders at him one more time before they turned the corner into the sanctuary.

Colleen stayed where she was. She glanced quickly at Patty then back to him. "So you're Mike, the guy with the car."

He would have preferred to be thought of with a more personal connection to Patty than the car, but at least it proved that she had talked about him to her friends to some degree. He was glad she hadn't referred to him as *the guy with the drinking problem.* "Yeah. That's me. The guy with the car."

Patty shuffled her feet. "Maybe we should go sit down. If you'll excuse us, Colleen?"

Mike followed Patty into the sanctuary where she selected a couple of seats near the back.

"I'm so surprised to see you here." Her cheeks darkened. "I mean, not that I'm not happy you came, because I certainly am. I just didn't think you'd come."

"Life is full of surprises, isn't it?"

"How did you get here?"

"I was a good boy and decided to save some money. Instead of taking a cab, I took the bus. They sure don't run very often Sunday morning, so I had to get up really early. I guess I had better get used to it, huh?"

All she did was stare at him. Before she could say any more, the lights dimmed, the volume of the band increased, a man at the front welcomed everyone present, and the congregation began to sing.

Mike didn't know the song, but he followed the words on the overhead screen. This church wasn't much different from the other one he'd been to a few times several years ago.

Everyone sat while the worship leader mentioned a few newsworthy items, including a tidbit about a woman who just had a baby. They paused for a short prayer, everyone stood, and the music continued.

He'd never paid attention to the words before, but this time he did. The message to the songs was simple and clear. One song in particular centered around grace, about God caring for every one of His children. Mike wanted to listen to the song again, but they moved on to the next one. He made a mental note to ask Patty after the service was over if that song in particular was available on CD.

When the songs were done, the pastor came to the front, welcomed everyone, and directed the congregation to open their Bibles and turn to the right verse.

He felt a nudge, so he leaned toward Patty.

She held her Bible open to the right place so he could read it with her. "Why didn't you bring that Bible I gave you?" she whispered.

"I've seen before how quickly everyone flips through to the right place during a service. I'd never find the right verse before everyone was finished reading it, so I thought I'd just sit back and listen."

The pastor read the verse and then began to expound on it, as well as a few others. The congregation and Patty faithfully flipped to the right place as soon as he mentioned another reference.

The pastor's voice boomed over the speakers. "John 3: 14–15 says, 'Just as Moses lifted up the snake in the desert, so the Son of Man must be lifted up, that everyone who believes in Him may have eternal life.' "

Mike stiffened in his chair. That verse was the one that he'd meant to ask Patty about, but he lost his place. He thought snakes were bad things when mentioned in the Bible, yet as far as he could tell, Jesus had just been compared to a snake.

The pastor continued, explaining that what Moses had actually lifted up wasn't a real snake but one made of bronze, and the point was that those who looked up at it as instructed, believing that they would live, lived. Likewise, those who believed in Jesus as their Savior were saved from punishment for their sins because of their belief. The issue wasn't the snake at all but having the faith to do what God said.

Mike sat with rapt attention, soaking in every word. It was as if the pastor's words of explanation and following practical application were meant just for him. A chill ran up his spine as he thought of watching Patty driving away last night, and how at the time he didn't know why he wanted to go to church today, only that he did.

Mike forced himself to breathe as he listened, not allowing himself to be distracted by anything going on around him. The pastor ended the sermon, everyone bowed their heads for another prayer, and the band at the front finished off the service with one last song.

The people around them rose and began to circulate and talk, but Mike remained seated. He wasn't in the mood to make small talk with strangers. A million thoughts cascaded through his mind.

"Well?" Patty asked beside him. "What did you think?"

Mike blinked and shook his head. "It was incredible. It was like he prepared that message just for me. That was the verse I wanted to ask you about and couldn't find. Aside from that, his sermon was easy to understand, the presentation was interesting. He didn't belabor the point too much, but still said all that was important to say. He made it so easy to understand. It sure didn't come together like that when I was reading it myself. I'm really glad I came. I learned a lot."

"Daddy is a very gifted speaker."

"He sure is. And he. . ." Mike's heart stopped, then pounded in his chest. "Daddy?"

"I wish I had the ability to deliver a message like that, but it's just not my gift."

His stomach tightened into a painful knot. "Daddy? The pastor is your father?"

"And every day he. . ." Her voice trailed off. "You mean you didn't know?"

He stared unseeingly at the empty podium. Most normal fathers didn't want him being in the same room with their daughters because he was such a bad influence, to say nothing of his reputation—especially in the past year. He could only imagine how much more so now that he was in trouble with the law.

Patty's father would never have been in trouble with the law, or with anything. Being a pastor, he'd probably never done a bad thing in his entire life.

He knew Patty had been raised in a pure and righteous home, but he had no idea it was that pure and righteous. He felt himself sink to a few levels below the common earthworm.

Mike thought he just might throw up. He was in love with the pastor's daughter.

# seven

"Mike? Are you okay?"

Patricia wanted to touch his forehead but didn't because of where they were. All the color had completely drained out of his face, and he was staring off into nothing.

He nodded, then shook his head. "Yeah, I'm fine. No. No, I'm not fine. I didn't know the pastor was your father. Why didn't you tell me?"

"I thought you knew."

She leaned back as Mike waved one hand in the air. "Of course I didn't know! How would I?"

"But you've spoken to Dad so many times. He even gave you my cell phone number, which he doesn't give out to just anybody."

He bowed his head and pinched the bridge of his nose, which Patricia didn't think was a good sign. "He calls you by your name, not by the title of Daughter."

"But what about Bruce?"

He still pinched the bridge of his nose, plus he shook his head. "That's a unique situation. We talk only about my personal life, not his—and especially not yours."

Patricia gritted her teeth, then stiffened in the chair. "Does it matter?" Most people knew she was the pastor's daughter before she met them for the first time. She didn't always like it, but she had become accustomed to living in her father's shadow. However, it was different when people got to know her first, especially out of church circles, and then found out she was a pastor's daughter. Then the reaction was often mixed. She saw it in people's eyes. Sometimes, the second they found out, suddenly she transformed from simply a nice

78

girl to some deity of angelic perfection, especially after they found out she worked for the church. She was no angel, far from it.

Some of the color returned to Mike's face. "I don't know if it matters. I don't want it to matter." He glanced nervously around the room, then flinched when he saw her father. "Let's get out of here. I'll take you to lunch."

Quickly, she gathered her purse and Bible and followed him into the parking lot. Rather than go to the usual church-crowd lunch hangout, they ended up at a pizzeria.

All went well until the group at the table next to them ordered a pitcher of beer. She saw Mike staring at it and wondered what was going through his mind. She couldn't personally fathom why anyone would continually drink to excess, knowing the damage it caused, especially after long-term abuse, but she couldn't deny that it happened. After listening to the speakers at the few AA meetings she'd been to, she wondered if many of the people really could say exactly why they drank so much, because every single one of them openly admitted that drinking only made things worse.

She didn't like the way Mike was staring at the beer. He wasn't even looking at the people. All his attention was focused on the pitcher. For whatever reason people had for drinking so much, it didn't take a rocket scientist to figure out that stress made the desire to drink stronger. And from his reaction when he found out about her father and the way he scooted out of the church when they saw him, she knew Mike was stressed.

"Mike? Do you want to go somewhere else?"

He shook his head, his ears reddened, and he turned to face her. "I'm sorry. No. I'm fine." He reached for the menu sitting in the middle of the table. "Let's order."

Curiously, not a word was said about her father, or the service, or anything about church or the Bible. She was dying to ask Mike what he found so captivating about her father's sermon because she had noticed that Mike was glued to her father's every word, but a voice in her heart told her to wait and bring up the subject at another time, after Mike had dealt with what he considered a shock. Restraint had never been one of her strengths, and every time a silence lulled in their conversation, Patricia struggled to let Mike speak first.

He said very little when she dropped him off at his house, so little that she was afraid to bring up the subject of returning his car.

Patricia decided that she would wait until Monday to return it, and since Monday was usually a slow day, a good time would be during her lunch break, since she knew she would be seeing Mike.

&

Patricia stood huddled in the church doorway, staring at the pouring rain. She didn't know how it happened, but instead of missing her little brown squirrel, she missed Mike.

She didn't want to miss Mike, but he had become such a regular part of her day, it felt odd that she was eating her sandwich without him.

A deep voice sounded behind her. "I guess he's not coming, is he?"

Patricia sighed. "No, Daddy, I wouldn't think so. He's only got his bike, and I've made such an issue about it being too expensive to take a cab, I know he won't do that just to sit and eat a sandwich beside me." Thunder rumbled in the distance. She sighed again. "He's definitely not coming."

"Bruce told me a little about him."

She tried not to cringe. She didn't know if that was good or bad, so she said nothing.

Her father stepped beside her, but didn't look at her. Instead, he also stared into the rain as he spoke. "It sounds like he has a lot of things to work out in his life."

"Yes, he does. And none of his friends are helping him. From what he says, none of them have called or offered any support; not one of them has invited him to go do something that doesn't involve drinking or going to their familiar hangouts. He must be so lonely, but on the surface, he's putting on a happy face. I know he's hurting deep down. He's just not letting it show."

"You be careful, Sweetheart. You don't have a lot of experience with people like him."

She turned toward her father. It was an echo of what Bruce had said. She wished she could pin the entire blame for her father's sentiments on Bruce, for tainting his opinion of Mike, but she couldn't. She was fully aware of her inexperience in these matters.

All her life, she rarely ventured out of church circles for both her social life and her job. She couldn't relate to Mike at all on many issues, and she knew he couldn't relate to her. Now that he knew the pastor was her father, the gap had widened even more. She realized that missing him now, the way she was, proved that being with him was more than a ministry. At some point it had become personal, and it shouldn't have.

"Daddy, am I doing the right thing?"

"I can't answer that. Have you prayed about it?"

"More than you can ever know."

"Then you're the one who can best answer that question."

She stared into the rain once more. "Bruce doesn't approve." She didn't want to ask for her father's approval, but she did want some kind of endorsement from him that she was doing the right thing.

"It's not up to me to approve or disapprove. This man is Bruce's client, and so Bruce sees this from a different perspective than you or I do. Bruce tends to see more failures in his line of work, and while I've seen a lot of heartache and tragedy in my time, I've also seen a lot of redemption in many people all else would have called hopeless. On the other hand, from a father's point of view, I don't want to see you hurt. But as a

Christian, I want to see Mike turn his life over to the love and care of Jesus, no matter how he's lived his life up to this point."

That was also what Patricia wanted to see. However, it was more than just as a Christian sister.

She couldn't deny the truth of what Bruce had pointed out. She was fully aware of many of Mike's shortcomings from her own personal dealings with him. Romans 3:23 echoed through her head.

"For all have sinned and fall short of the glory of God."

In God's eyes, she was no different. For all her faith and good works, she was still a sinner, but she was justified by the blood of Jesus. More than anything, she wanted Mike to be justified, too.

All her life, she had been spared from much of the heartache she saw around her. She had been raised in a wonderful home, full of love and support, surrounded by friends and family as well as the whole church, teaching her not only of God's love but also how to show God's love to others. She didn't know what kind of love or support network Mike had grown up with, but he needed someone to support him and push him in the right direction now. The second half of Luke 12:48 flashed through her mind.

"From everyone who has been given much, much will be demanded; and from the one who has been entrusted with much, much more will be asked."

She had indeed been given much, and it was now her turn to give much back.

Patricia turned to face her father.

She didn't say anything, but he nodded slowly, once.

"I'll be praying for both of you," he said.

Patricia returned to her desk. She also had a lot of praying to do. Tonight was Mike's special meeting with Claude's group, and they would be doing step two. She pulled the little AA pamphlet out of her drawer and read it.

*(2) Came to believe that a Power greater than ourselves*

*could restore us to sanity.*

Quickly, she shoved it back into her drawer. She didn't know who was more insane, Mike or herself.

All day long, that one sentence echoed through her head. Even on the short drive home, she still couldn't get it out of her head or the ramifications of how it related to Mike.

Lunch had felt strange. Except for the few minutes she'd spent with her father, it was the first time in a week she'd been alone at lunchtime. Usually she ate her dinner alone, but today it felt strange being alone in the kitchen. In order to shake the sensation, she ate her dinner in front of the television—something she never did.

When something disturbed her, she always pulled out her Bible and paged through and read her highlighted verses until something jumped out at her, and then she read the surrounding section. She couldn't even do that, because she had given the Bible containing all her notes to Mike.

In less than two weeks, the man had invaded every portion of her life.

She had just decided to go to bed when the phone rang.

"Hi, Patty. Busy?"

"Hi, Mike. What's up?"

"I just got home from that meeting at Claude's house, and I really needed to do something normal, so I had to call you."

She wouldn't have called starting a phone conversation at ten at night normal. "Uh-huh," she mumbled, waiting for him to continue.

"It was a very strange meeting. For most of it we talked about all the stupid things we've all done over the years. You know, the insanity of it all. In the middle of the meeting, we all laughed about it, but really, it wasn't very funny when you think of it. We're all supposed to be responsible adults. It really made me think. At the end, we came to the part you probably want to hear about. We talked about how God could help us. And I really believe that He can."

Her heart pounded. "That's great."

"I'm just not sure that He would want to. I haven't exactly been a prime candidate."

"God loves you, Mike. Really. Why do you think He's put you among those people? And He did it before any real harm was done."

She heard him suck in a deep intake of breath. "I guess."

Silence hung on the line.

"I guess I should let you go," Mike mumbled.

She couldn't completely stifle a yawn. "Yes, it's late. Are you going to come and visit me at lunch time tomorrow?"

His voice brightened. "Depends on the weather, but to be with you is worth the risk of catching pneumonia."

Patricia harumphed. "I don't think so. See you if the weather holds."

When she went to bed, she found herself praying for good weather, just because she wanted to see her little squirrel again.

In the morning, her prayers were answered. It was a lovely day. The air was fresh and clean, the birds were singing, and the drops of water beaded and glistened off the pristine wax finish of Mike's car.

She hummed as she worked and then went outside for lunch early.

Mike joined her at precisely noon.

"No chipmunk today?"

"Yes, the squirrel was here. You scared it away again."

He emptied a sandwich, a couple of wrapped cookies, and a few pieces of bread out of his backpack. When all was laid out between them on the bench, he turned to her and grinned. "It'll probably come back. This time I'm ready."

She wasn't so sure the squirrel would return, but she didn't want to contradict him because she didn't know what he was trying to do, attract the squirrel or impress her by bribing the squirrel.

Since neither of them had started eating, Patricia paused for a prayer of thanks over their lunch, and they began to eat. Unlike most days, this time Mike was strangely silent. Patricia remained quiet, waiting for him to talk first, which he eventually did when he was almost finished with his sandwich.

"There's something I've got to tell you."

She nodded and waited.

"Yesterday, on the phone, when you said that so far, no real harm was done because of, well, you know."

Again, Patricia remained silent while Mike sorted out what he felt was so important to tell her. She had a feeling that a confession was coming, even though she had not asked for one.

"Well, that's not quite true. You already know that I left the scene of an accident, but that wasn't so bad. His insurance covered it and stuff. What I have to tell you is that I was engaged once. I didn't treat her very well. She ended up losing her job because of me."

Patricia tried not to show her shock. She didn't know what hit her harder, that someone had lost their job because of something he'd done or that Mike had once loved someone so much that he had planned to marry her.

"I know she would have gotten another job quick enough. She was more than capable, and my dad gave her a good severance package—something he sure didn't give me. But now I know what it's like to get fired, and it's not a very good feeling. I'm not having as easy a time as I thought finding another job, either. Last week I thought I had something, but as soon as I told my prospective employer that I'd need some time off for my pending court case, they were suddenly no longer interested."

She stared blankly at him, trying to let it all sink in. Her brief experience with Mike had shown that he could pour on the charm when he wanted to, but deep down, he wasn't a bad guy. Knowing that once he had planned to marry someone contradicted her playboy image of him. The woman must have been very special to make him decide to settle down, and Patricia also wondered what had happened that caused them to split up.

"Do you still see her?" She was afraid to know the answer, but some sick part of her had to know.

"No. I haven't seen her since the breakup. It was rather unpleasant for both of us, and it was entirely my fault."

Patricia remained silent, afraid to ask, and not sure it was any of her business.

Mike turned his head, not looking at her as he spoke. "I was cheating on her. I was a jerk."

The bite of her sandwich became a lump of cardboard in her mouth. She swallowed it painfully and dropped the uneaten remainder of the sandwich into the container.

Mike did the same. "It still bugs me, and it's been three years. It was the stupidest thing I've ever done in my life."

Patricia stared blankly at the trees.

He swiped what was left of his lunch into his backpack, except for one of cookies, which he slid on the bench toward her. "I think I'd better go."

Without another word he slung his backpack over his shoulder, strode to his bike, and rode off.

Patricia watched the street long after he'd gone.

His words echoed in her head. He had said it was the stupidest thing he'd ever done. It shouldn't have mattered to her, because Mike was only supposed to be a ministry to her. God trusted her to guide Mike, to show him God's love, and God had orchestrated the timing to be when Mike needed it the most.

But it did matter. Her throat tightened, and her eyes burned. Mike was still in love with his ex-fiancée.

❧

Mike slammed the door behind him and kicked his sneakers off, not caring that he hit the wall with them, stomped into the living room, and flopped down on the couch.

He'd blown it. As soon as he told Patty he'd been engaged once, he'd seen a change come over her. But when he admitted that he'd been cheating on Robbie—that was when he knew anything he'd ever hoped for was over.

But it was something she had to know. He knew there was no way she'd ever learn that from Bruce, because he hadn't told Bruce. They didn't talk about personal details of his past that weren't directly related to his drinking habits.

For now, Patty wasn't going to meet any of his friends, but that wasn't to say it would never happen. He didn't think it was likely that he would bump into Robbie on the street when he was with Patty, but the future possibility of either existed.

He didn't want her to find out that way; therefore, he told her himself in what he hoped would be the least damaging way. He had expected her to be shocked, but he hadn't expected utter disdain.

Considering her upbringing, he could only imagine what she thought of him being unfaithful to the woman he was supposed to marry, which was the most important commitment a person would ever make.

He'd handled himself badly. He still didn't know why he had cheated on Robbie, because it had started so innocently. Suzie had started it, taunting and tempting him, and at first he'd simply flirted back, the same as he always did, but Suzie had kept at him. Before he realized what was happening, he was seeing Suzie on the side. If he'd been half a man, he would have broken up with Robbie then, by telling her they weren't as suited as he originally thought, or he would have told Suzie to get lost, but he hadn't. The whole thing had fed his ego, and he'd made the most of it at the time, or so he thought.

Then Robbie had come in to work early and caught him with Suzie. The scene that followed had been so horrible that he'd fallen into what he could now see as a pit of self-indulgence. For a while, he'd been into such substance abuse that there were holes in his memory. There were days that he couldn't remember where he was or what he'd done. Looking back, he almost couldn't believe he had been so stupid, that he actually could remember some of the things he'd done that were less than noble. He'd let everything spiral completely out of control. He'd lived his life going from one party to the next.

Except, he wasn't having a lot of fun. His life had no meaning. He had accomplished nothing. He now had the possibility of a jail sentence to look forward to, and it was his own fault. It wasn't just himself whom he had hurt. First, he'd hurt Robbie, both emotionally and financially, and now he'd physically hurt the man whose car he ran into. He'd run from the results both times.

Mike sat up on the couch and buried his face in his hands, speaking out loud. "God, if You're out there, and if You're listening to me, I'm sorry for the things I've done and the mess I've made. Please, I beg You to forgive me. And if You can, please help me make things right with Patty. I've blown it once. I don't want to blow it again. Lord God, she's so special. Show me how to treat her right."

He sat in silence, not moving. Today was Tuesday, and he knew that Tuesday nights Patty went to Bible study meetings.

He stood and walked into his bedroom, picking up Patty's Bible from the nightstand where he'd tossed it earlier. He'd asked God to help him, both to straighten himself out as well as to help him in building a relationship with Patty. If he was going to ask such things, then he thought it only fair to study God's word and to learn more about the God Who supposedly loved him as much as Patty said.

Without putting the Bible down, he walked to the phone and dialed the church. Of course, Patty's cheerful voice answering made his pulse quicken.

"Hey, Patty. I've been thinking. You said you go to Bible study meetings on Tuesday nights. It's Tuesday, and I'd like to go. Am I invited?"

# eight

Mike smiled a greeting as he shook hands with Gary and his wife, Melinda, the people who led the home Bible study meeting, and then made himself comfortable on the couch. As he hoped, Patty sat beside him.

Everyone present was looking at them. In people's minds, officially, they were together, and he liked it that way. To further enforce their assumption, he laid his hand over Patty's, patted it, then returned his hand to the Bible in his lap as he laughed at a joke someone made while they were waiting.

They were about to start when one more couple arrived, and everyone shuffled over to make room, which was fine with him because that meant Patty had to sit right up against him. When Mike looked up at the new arrivals, his heart skipped a beat.

It was Bruce and his wife. It hadn't occurred to Mike that Bruce would be here. He had assumed that the crowd would be made up of Patty's friends. He didn't think about her brother.

Bruce smiled at everyone as he apologized for being late, but when Bruce looked at him, Mike could see a falter in the smile and a hesitation in Bruce's movements. No one else appeared to notice, but Mike was positive he hadn't imagined it.

Just as Patty had warned him, they opened with a shared prayer after Gary asked everyone present if they had any prayer requests. Mike had a few concerns, but he wasn't going to share them with this group of strangers, and he especially wasn't going to share them with Patty, because most of them were about her.

The lesson was informative and done in a casual presentation that Mike could relate to. Questions and comments were invited, and Mike remained silent while he listened. He was receiving enough information to process without asking for more.

Last night the group at Claude's meeting was completely different. They were all people much like himself; a couple of them believed in God; most of them didn't. One thing they all believed was that there was some greater power out there that could help them make a break from the addiction they all shared.

Tonight, many present, like Patty and Bruce, had been raised in homes where Christian values were taught and believing in God was never a question, God was always there. Like Patty, he didn't think any of them had ever had anything really bad happen to them, yet they depended on God anyway. A few people were present who made their decisions as adults, and even though it was hard to tell what had made them make the decision to become Christians, their belief and faith were strong.

Either way, everything that was read or commented on showed that God loved everyone, no matter what kind of people they were or what they were doing at that point in their lives. Mike found it fascinating, and he had to admire every one of them for standing up for what they believed.

When the study part of the meeting was finished, they all chatted as they helped themselves to coffee, tea, and some wonderful homemade cookies. Everyone talked to him except Bruce, which left him feeling strangely relieved.

On the way home, he wanted to go out for coffee or somewhere he could talk privately with Patty without her feeling intimidated, which she would have at his house. Even though it was his car, he wasn't driving and he couldn't protest when she took him straight home, making it very clear that she had no intention of coming in.

After his disclosure earlier today, he could see a difference in the way Patty treated him. It wasn't overtly noticeable, but she had erected a wall between them, and he had to find a way to break it down. It did encourage him that she had taken him with her tonight without complaint, which he hoped was a step in the right direction.

Once he was at home alone, Mike couldn't quell a feeling of agitation. Any other day, he would have poured himself a drink and parked himself in front of the television, but that wasn't an option. For a complete change of pace, in order to keep his mind busy, he turned the CD player on loud and played a few games on his computer. When he got bored, he did something he had never done before, which was to wash his kitchen floor since he no longer had a housekeeper to do it for him. He then vacuumed the entire house. After that, he dug through the fridge to see if there was anything worthwhile to eat.

Nothing soothed him.

Despite it being earlier than his usual bedtime, he decided to hit the sack early. As he reached for the light, he saw Patty's Bible lying where he'd left it, and instead of turning off the light, he picked up the Bible. This time, instead of paging through for the highlighted parts, Mike started at the beginning of the book of Genesis and read until his eyes would no longer focus. Then he drifted off to sleep.

He woke to the sound of birds twittering, which meant only one thing. It wasn't raining, and he would be joining Patty for lunch.

After a few unprofitable calls for jobs listed in the help wanted ads, Mike needed to do something to ease his frustration. A long bike ride was the perfect solution. He made and packed himself a lunch, including a couple of pieces of bread for the squirrel, and was on his way.

This time, as he leaned his bike against the church wall, instead of rushing across the grass to greet Patty, he stood in the shadows and watched her from a distance.

First she checked her watch, then emptied her lunch containers from the bag onto the bench, paused to pray, and took

a bite of her sandwich. Then she tore a piece of bread off the
extra piece she always brought and looked into the trees,
waiting for the squirrel. Just looking at her calmed him and
made him smile. She was kind and gentle, yet had a mind of
her own, and held no hesitation or second thoughts to do what
it took to keep him in line. No woman had ever made him
want to stay in line until he met Patty.

Mike sucked in a deep breath, hooked his thumbs into the
straps of his backpack, and walked quickly across the grass.
Just as he started on his path, the little brown squirrel began
to approach Patty. It was too late to turn back, and even
though he slowed his pace, the squirrel turned and fled.

"Hi, Mike," she called out without turning around.

Mike smiled. He wondered what she would do if one day it
wasn't he who approached. The thought caused a knot to form
in his stomach. He didn't want anyone else to approach her.

"I think I scared your chipmunk again," he said as he sat
beside her on the bench.

She grumbled something he couldn't understand.

He tried to keep a straight face. "Pardon me? Sorry, I
couldn't quite hear you."

"I said it's a *squirrel*. It has a long bushy tail. It's a solid
color. It's a *squirrel*."

"Shh. Don't raise your voice so much. You'll scare it away."

"You've already done that," she mumbled under her breath.

Mike laughed and emptied his backpack. He held out a
cookie toward her, waving it in the air. "I brought you a treat,
but it's bound to be a disappointment after those wonderful
cookies last night."

He held it in front of her, sweeping it in the air under her
nose until she took it from his hand.

"You're welcome," he said, still grinning.

"Thank you," she grumbled.

He continued to tease her and tell jokes until she couldn't
help but smile at him. The squirrel finally did return, and he

sat completely still and silent while she fed it. Mike marveled at how a wild animal could be lured so close, even though he knew the answer. The same gentle spirit that drew the squirrel also drew him.

They stood at the same time when her lunch break was over. Mike slung his backpack over his shoulders and picked up her bag after she had deposited her empty containers into it.

With his heart in his throat, he grasped her hand and held onto it and, without saying a word, gave her a slight pull to start her walking back across the field and to the building. To his delight, she didn't pull her hand away as they walked together. He couldn't believe how wonderful it felt, something so simple as holding hands, compared to some of the things he'd done in the past with women he'd dated. Most of them, however, were far from pure, and their words and actions only showed what was in their hearts, and that was that they were as self-centered as he was. There had been times lately that he had come out of a relationship feeling used, and that wasn't the way it was supposed to be. A man and a woman were to cherish each other and treat the other with respect and dignity.

It was a bitter reminder that he didn't deserve a woman like Patty.

When they arrived back at the building, she stood with him until he mounted his bike. He wanted to kiss her so badly he was grateful for the distraction of holding the handlebars.

"Good-bye, Mike."

"Yeah. See you tomorrow."

She opened her mouth but then closed it again. His gut clenched to think that she could have been ready to tell him not to come back. He rode off before she had the chance to think about it. He planned to be back to share her lunch break, not only tomorrow, but every day.

꙳

Mike touched up the gel in his hair and pulled his jacket out of the closet. Last night his friend Wayne had called to remind him that tonight was the annual car and truck show, and everyone had asked if he was coming this year. Of course, he was thrilled to be asked. He was very much looking forward to going.

He hadn't seen his friends and had barely even talked to them since he'd been arrested. Seeing Patty nearly every day had helped him when he felt left out of their activities, but now that he'd made plans to spend the next day without her, he almost regretted it, because he knew he would miss her. He'd missed her terribly on Monday when it had rained, but he'd seen her for lunch every other day. And on Friday afternoon, when he was about to call her to see if she would spend the evening with him, Bruce had called unexpectedly to take him to an AA meeting, which he couldn't refuse. What he had really wanted to do was to take Patty out, and today, now that Wayne would be there any minute to pick him up, he wished that instead of Wayne, it was Patty who was coming to get him.

Mike shook his head. Even married men had to have a night or two out with the guys, and he wasn't even close to being married to Patty, no matter how much he wished he could be.

The thought nearly caused him to stumble. He did want to be married to Patty, but wasn't in a position to ask, even if he thought there was the slightest possibility that she would say yes. Now that he'd told her what a jerk he'd been when he was engaged before, he doubted she would consider it. After all, who would ever want to set themselves up for heartbreak?

A horn honked in the driveway, so Mike set the house alarm, locked up, and jogged to Wayne's car. After they picked up their other three friends, they were on their way.

They laughed and had a great time, joking around all the way to the arena. The only thing Mike thought missing in the conversation was that for such old-time friends, they didn't talk about anything important. Even Wayne, who was supposed to be his best friend, didn't ask him how he'd been over the last few weeks, nor did he ask what AA meetings were like. Most of all, Mike wanted an opening to tell them that he'd done some thinking and to tell them that throughout all that had happened, he felt a deep inner peace knowing that somehow God was in charge, and everything was going to be fine.

Soon they were mingling with the crowd, making the rounds touring all the new cars and trucks, and checking out most of the booths hawking automotive accessories of every imaginable description and possible use.

After stuffing themselves silly with corn dogs and French fries, Mike wanted to go to the other building and check out what was there, but on their way, they came to the beer garden.

His friends wanted to go in, because every year they made the beer garden the crowning glory of the whole auto show experience.

Mike froze. He didn't come here to drink. He came here to have a good time and look at the new cars and the latest toys that went with them. Sure, in previous years he had enjoyed the beer garden, but this year it wasn't on his agenda.

Apparently, none of his friends had considered that.

Travis gleefully announced the absence of a line and was the first one to enter, then Wayne and Rick. Dave hesitated, but only for a minute.

When he didn't move, Dave pulled him by the arm. "Come on, Mikey, old boy. If you're really on the wagon, you can have a soda."

Mike didn't want to sit in the beer garden and drink soft drinks while everyone else around him got drunk.

At his silence, Wayne nudged him. "This way, you can be the designated driver."

Mike stiffened. They had never had a designated driver before. Warning bells went off in his head. To his friends, his arrest may have served as a warning about getting caught drinking and driving, not about actually cutting back on their drinking habits. It dawned on him that the only reason he'd been asked to come with them was because they knew he was going to stay sober, and they wanted him to drive. "I can't be the designated driver. My license was suspended, remember?"

Travis patted him on the back. "Who cares? No one will catch you. Just drive the speed limit and stop for all the stop signs. Nothing will happen."

Mike backed up a step. While he knew that if he carefully obeyed every little rule of the road, the chances of getting stopped on a busy Saturday night were next to non-existent; that wasn't the point. He had lost his license for a valid reason, and he fully intended to obey every restriction imposed upon him.

"No," he said bluntly.

Travis patted him on the back again, then nudged him to start walking into the beer garden. "Aw, come on, buddy. You wouldn't want us to get caught or get in an accident because we were a little over the legal limit, would you?"

Mike stopped dead in his tracks and smacked Travis's arm away. He knew what they had in mind. It wasn't to be a little over the legal blood-alcohol limit. They planned to be a lot over the legal limit. "This is blackmail."

"It's not blackmail. We're your friends."

He turned to Wayne. "And what would happen if I did get stopped, was arrested again, and your car was impounded? What would you do then?"

Wayne shrugged his shoulders. "That's not going to happen."

Mike clenched his teeth. No one thought it would happen to them, but sometimes it did. He never could have foreseen what had happened to him, but things like that happened all the time to people.

"No."

"Coward."

"I'm not driving. You guys are making a big mistake."

His friends, including his very best friend, Wayne, started quietly clucking like chickens.

"I don't need this. You guys are on your own." He turned and strode away into the crowd, ignoring their rude comments behind him as he walked. He didn't stop until he was outside.

Mike drew a deep breath of the cool night air into his lungs, but it didn't relieve the numb feeling inside. These were his friends. Every year they went to the auto show together, and every year they had a good time.

He leaned against the building, out of sight from other people going in and out of the door. That was all he ever did with his friends, have a good time. Thinking back, though, he couldn't really recall exactly what was so fun.

This year, in order to have their fun, his friends had planned this—to take advantage of him. What hurt the worst was their attempt at manipulation, trying to lay a guilt trip on him to get him to drive them home. By using his refusal to drink, the rest of them planned to get drunker than usual. They had seemed more chipper on the way there than usual, and now he knew why.

A couple of months ago, he would have been angry at being set up, but he wasn't angry. Yes, he was hurt, but more than anything, he felt sorry for them that they would go to such means to get drunk. They weren't going to have as good a time as they thought if they couldn't remember the next day what they'd done. Also, no matter how "good" a time they had, their alleged fun would not be worth the hangover. He'd been that route himself enough times to know. But then again, it never stopped him from over-indulging, nor was it likely to stop his friends today.

He was not going to give in and break the law or disobey the conditions of his probation so his friends could continue to drink. Any efforts to convince them to skip the beer garden and simply cruise the auto show, which was what they came for in the first place, would be fruitless. Their barbed comments behind his back on his way out foretold that nothing would be different upon his return.

Mike looked down the street. It had gotten dark hours ago, and even though he was in reasonably good shape and he was tall enough not to be considered an easy mark, this was not the best area of town to be out alone late at night, even for a physically fit grown man.

He unclipped his cell phone from his belt and began to dial Patty's number but stopped before he hit the last digit. He'd called her to bail him out when he had to pick up his car, but he wasn't going to inconvenience her again, especially so late on a Saturday night. Nor did he want to further humiliate himself by asking her to come all this way and rescue him after his so-called friends had abandoned him. Instead, he hit the clear button and returned the phone to his belt.

Mike checked his wallet only to discover that he didn't have enough money for a cab. He again looked down the street, ran his fingers through his hair, straightened his back, and headed for the nearest bus stop.

Being alone for so long waiting for the bus at night gave Mike time to think. After two transfers, and after regularly checking his wristwatch, he estimated the amount of time that his friends would be at the beer garden before they were asked to leave. From his seat in the back of the bus, he called directory assistance for the non-emergency number, and dialed the police.

"Hello? I'd like to report a drunk driver."

After he completed the call, he closed his eyes and prayed, knowing that even though Wayne would probably hate him, he had done the right thing.

# nine

Patricia spread her lunch out on the park bench but didn't open anything. Mike was late, but she was positive he was going to be there.

Once again, she checked the time. She hoped he was going to be there.

He had phoned early Sunday morning and asked her to pick him up for church. Of course she couldn't turn him down. In the past month, she had seen amazing growth in Mike. She could see his perception changing, opening a little more every week to God's wisdom and leading. All day long on Sunday he'd been uncharacteristically quiet, and when he finally did speak, he had asked some very strange questions about friendship.

The best she could do on short notice was to show him the loyal friendship between David and Jonathan. When she asked why he was asking, he became evasive, which made her interpret his questions as a hint that he had decided to simply be friends and nothing more.

Being friends was also what Patricia knew was best, but against her better judgment, she wanted more than friendship with Mike. It wasn't going to happen, nor would it have been right in their given situation. All her counseling training and experience taught her that after a trauma or upheaval in a person's life, major decisions, especially matters of the heart, should be avoided until a significant amount of time had passed. Not only that, it was clear to Patricia that Mike still carried a torch for his ex-fiancée.

He'd also been very quiet when he joined her for lunch Monday. If he still hadn't snapped out of his doldrums today, she planned to ask him what was wrong.

This time she saw him coming before the squirrel showed up for his daily treat. Today she anticipated him telling her all about the special Monday evening meeting at Claude's house.

"Sorry I'm late. You should have started eating without me. This morning I was talking to Claude on the phone since he had the day off, and before I knew it, it was past time to leave." He shucked his backpack and sat beside her. "The meeting last night was great." He began to remove his lunch from his backpack.

She opened her mouth to ask him about it, but he started before she could make a sound.

"The step of the night was *'Made a decision to turn our will and our lives over to the care of God as we understood Him.'* And you know what? I did that, and I feel great."

He grinned ear-to-ear, and Patricia could see that he wasn't exaggerating. He looked great, unlike the quiet and somber person he'd been over the last two days. Today he was a different person.

"After the meeting was over and everyone left, I stayed and prayed with Claude, and it's like the weight of the world has been lifted from my shoulders." Instead of doing what she expected, which was to start eating his lunch, Mike enclosed both her hands in his. "God loves me, Patty. He cared for me even when I didn't care about Him. He's kept me safe, and He put you in my life. He put Claude in my life, and I don't believe that any of this is an accident. Most of all, Jesus has already taken the punishment for everything I've done. Just because He loves me."

Patricia stared at Mike. He radiated pure joy, and she thought her heart would burst with happiness for him. He had Jesus in his heart, and it showed. The only thing about being with him now that wasn't perfect was a tiny twinge of resentment that he hadn't made his decision with her, but she quickly pushed such thinking aside.

"And even if I do have to go to jail for a short time, I can handle that. I did wrong, and I still have to face the consequences of my actions. But from here on, I'm a new creation."

*Jail*. The word echoed in Patricia's mind, crashing into her heart. Spending time in jail was still a very real possibility for Mike. For today, he was living in a euphoric bubble, but as life returned to normal, daily routine would bring him back down to earth a little bit. She said a quick prayer in her head that Mike would never lose the enthusiasm she saw right now.

"I want to celebrate. I've never felt like this before."

She looked down at their joined hands, then back up to his face. She knew he still had more money than she did, despite his current unemployment status. However, he had shared with her that every time he thought he was close to getting a job, no one wanted to take the chance of hiring him before his court date, in case he had to go to jail. If that were the case, and if that trend continued, his money was going to run very low, very fast, especially if he did get a jail sentence.

The entrance of a new soul into God's Kingdom was the best reason for celebration there could ever be, both in heaven and on earth, no matter what unpleasantness lay in the future. For this, Patty wanted to celebrate with him, and for this, it would be her treat. "I think a celebration is a great idea." At her words, she felt an encouraging gentle squeeze on her hands.

She figured he would choose a convenient evening and name an expensive restaurant she probably couldn't afford, but she would treat him anyway. "What do you want to do?" she asked.

Slowly, he released her hands and gently cupped her face, cradling her chin between both palms. His voice dropped to a low rumble. "I want to kiss you."

Before she could protest or think of a good reason why not, he leaned forward over their lunches spread between them on the park bench and kissed her. He kissed her slowly and fully and so sweetly it made her insides melt.

No one had ever kissed her like this. Her stomach fluttered, and her heart pounded. Then he broke the contact, let his hands drop, and it was over.

Patricia sat speechless. Gradually, a lazy and very self-satisfied smile came over his face, making him more handsome than any man had a right to be. "I've wanted to do that for a long time."

Patricia blinked herself back to reality and abruptly reached for her sandwich container. Not that she was hungry anymore, but she suddenly, desperately needed something to do.

A quick movement near the front of the bench caught her attention. She turned her head just in time to see the little brown squirrel run off into the trees.

She had forgotten about the squirrel, and this time it was her own movement that sent him scurrying away.

Mike made a strange choking sound and bit his bottom lip, like he was trying very hard not to laugh. "You scared Charlie Chipmunk."

She stared at him, not caring that her mouth was hanging open. She couldn't think of a single response. She couldn't even remind him that it was a squirrel.

"Don't you think we should pray and start eating? You have to get back to the office soon."

"Yes. Of course." Because he was a new child in Christ, she wanted to reach out and hold his hands while they prayed, but she was afraid to touch him. Since she already had her sandwich container in her hand, she opened it and laid it and the lid on the bench, then opened her juice container, as well as the plastic container containing some fruit cocktail, and spread everything out between them. The open containers, plus lids, effectively doubled the space between them.

"I think today you should pray," Patricia mumbled. She folded her hands in her lap and waited. She knew she was being immature, but she couldn't think properly.

"I'm not very good at this, but I know God knows what's in

my heart." Mike cleared his throat and they both bowed their heads. "Dear Lord God. I thank You for this good lunch. And for Patty. Thank You for putting her into my life. Thanks for this special private place where we meet every day. Thank You most of all for Your love and for Your Son, Jesus. Amen."

"Amen," she said, then picked up her sandwich.

Mike also bit into his sandwich, and then talked around the food in his mouth. "I didn't have time to check it out, but did you know they're expanding the mall down the street?"

Patricia listened to him make cheerful conversation while they ate together, but for once she did very little talking. All she could think of was how Mike had kissed her. She tried to figure out why he would have done that, but the only thing she could think of was that he was so excited about his new-found discovery of God's love for him that he acted impulsively, and since she was the nearest person, his enthusiasm spilled over onto her.

She wanted to talk to Bruce about what exactly was said at those meetings Mike attended, but lately Bruce had been very touchy whenever the subject of Mike came up. Since Sunday, she found herself avoiding Bruce, because she knew he would give her a rough time when he discovered that she still had Mike's car.

If she couldn't get the information out of Bruce, she would have to go elsewhere. Even though she didn't know Claude except for the two times they'd met, Patricia decided to call him. She had no intention of prodding for confidential details of what Mike said at the meetings, because that was meant to stay within the boundaries of their meeting and was only for the ears of those who attended.

She needed to know that the things Claude was teaching Mike were spiritually sound. To do that, she needed an excuse to talk to him and broach the subject.

Because Mike had been a little late arriving, the lunch break seemed the shortest of her life, added to the fact that

Mike was talking nonstop.

On the hour, she stacked her empty lunch containers in her bag at the same time as Mike tossed his empty containers into his backpack.

Mike stood and slung the backpack over his shoulders. "Oh, before I forget. Remember that this Thursday is Claude's seven-year cake, and you said we'd go to his special meeting."

Patricia couldn't hold back her smile. God knew the answer before she had formulated the question.

She very much looked forward to talking to Claude.

&

"Patty! Mike! Good to see you two!"

Patricia smiled politely while Claude first pumped Mike's hand, then laid one hand on Mike's shoulder and patted him on the back with the other. She had always found it amusing the lengths men would go to not to hug each other, even when the situation warranted it. The bond between Mike and Claude was almost tangible, and her heart filled with joy for both of them.

Since Claude was busy talking to a great many people, Patricia did not protest when Mike led her to a chair, and they sat down to wait for the meeting to start.

This time, Patricia found the meeting slightly different. The few meetings she'd previously attended hadn't had a specific theme. Often the speakers didn't know what they were going to say until they got to the front; in fact, some of the speakers didn't know they were going to speak until they felt led to say something at that particular moment.

Today, many of the people present included Claude in their testimonies, either congratulating him for this, his anniversary of seven years without a drink, or saying what a help Claude had been to them in their individual quests for sobriety.

Claude came to the podium last. He briefly told of the happenings around his decision to begin attending AA meetings, and spoke of a man who had greatly helped him in the beginning. Her heart filled with joy for him when Claude elaborated on what AA circles called his "spiritual awakening." His experience was very much like what Mike had gone through; first there was a general belief in God as a Supreme Creator, but this grew to a more personal relationship as he realized the full scope of God's love in his life, despite the bad things that had happened. He gave all the credit for his accomplishments to Jesus, and at the end of his testimony, the crowd burst into rounds of applause. Brief glances to the sides showed Patricia that she was the only one with tears in her eyes. Quickly she wiped them away before anyone could notice.

When the meeting came to a close, Claude served everyone a piece of the largest Black Forest cake Patricia had ever seen. Since he was the center of attention today, she chose not to question him. Besides, many of her questions on where he stood spiritually were answered from listening to his testimony.

With a piece of cake in hand, she retreated to an empty spot in the room with Mike.

Mike stuffed the last of his cake into his mouth and swiped away a bit of icing from his chin. "Claude just asked me if I wanted to go to church with him on Sunday. I told him that I've been going with you, and then he said you were welcome to come, too. You want to?"

Her first thought was to decline because she handed out bulletins with her mother, but she couldn't talk with cake in her mouth. Before she could form the words, another thought struck her. Last Sunday, when she had made the rounds amongst the congregation with Mike at her side, she had been very aware of Bruce nearby, and she got the impression that he hadn't been very pleased to see her with Mike. Nothing had been said, but his disapproval weighed heavily on her long after church was over. She didn't like confrontations, especially since she'd already told Bruce that she knew what she was doing by spending so much time with Mike.

Even after that, Bruce's attitude apparently did not change. Not that she would skip church to get away from Bruce, but attending another church for one Sunday was a rare opportunity for her, and it gave her an excuse to avoid her brother.

Patricia nodded and swallowed. "Yes. I'd like that."

Mike smiled, making Patricia's foolish heart flutter. "Great. I'll get the address from him. As usual, you'll have to pick me up."

She knew she should have given him back his car long ago, but with her own car still needing that rather expensive repair, using Mike's car was too convenient. Besides, many of the miles she put on his car were from chauffeuring him around, so that made it acceptable for her to still have it.

She smiled back. "Name the time, and I'll be there."

ᘔ

"Hi, Patty." Mike shucked off his backpack, dusted off the bench so he wouldn't have to send his good slacks to the dry cleaner, and sat.

Patty's eyes narrowed slightly as she checked out his clothes. She turned her head to look for his bike which was exactly in the same spot as he parked it every day. "Why are you dressed like that?"

He sighed and ran one hand down the lapel of his suit jacket. Since it was his turn to bring lunch, he couldn't be late. He only had time to throw everything into his backpack before he rushed out the door. "I didn't have time to change. I went for a job interview this morning, and I got home five minutes after the time I should have left to come here.

"I wouldn't have minded you being late. Really. But you do look nice in the suit. How did it go?"

Mike sighed. "The same as last time. It looked really promising, but as soon as I told them about needing time off for court, they suddenly didn't think I was suitable."

"Don't worry, you'll get something soon."

"I don't know. I'm not so sure anymore." He sighed again. "Let's eat." He emptied all the containers from his backpack onto the bench between them, they paused for a prayer of thanks for the food, then dug in.

"If you were running late, I would have understood. All you had to do was phone, and I could have picked something up at the local drive-thru."

Mike grinned. "Honestly, I had everything made and wrapped before I had to leave for the interview. I just had to throw everything into my backpack and go."

The smile she gave him did funny things to his hungry stomach. "I didn't know you were so organized."

He held up a brown paper bag. "Hey. I even brought lunch for the chipmunk."

She rolled her eyes. "It's a squirrel. One day I'll bring an encyclopedia and show you the genus and species."

Mike laughed and bit into his sandwich. Today he appreciated the teasing because it distracted him from what was really on his mind. He had wanted to tell Patty that he'd gotten a job, because he really thought he had it. Now, after yet another failure, he was more than disappointed; he was downright discouraged. He usually didn't give up when he was going after something he wanted, but this time he didn't see any point in continuing to look for a job until after the court case was over and whatever sentence he received was over.

He was about to point out that her little critter still hadn't shown up when he heard muffled footsteps on the path to the bench. They both looked up at the same time.

"It's Daddy." Patty checked her watch. "I wonder what he wants."

Mike's chest tightened. He often chatted briefly with Patty's father after Sunday services, but it was always only pleasant small talk, nothing personal, only stuff suitable for discussion within the congregation. A few times, Mike had spoken to her father on the phone while waiting for Patty to answer, but that had been simply passing time, and there was never time or opportunity for a serious discussion. He'd only been inside the church on a weekday a couple of times because usually he joined Patty at the bench.

Now there was only the three of them, no one else anywhere nearby, no time constraints, and no distractions.

Patty leaned slightly closer. With her father approaching, he didn't want it to appear that he was too close to her, but he didn't want to look guilty by backing away too quickly. He forced himself to be still.

Patty's voice dropped to a whisper. "I'll bet Daddy will be impressed with the suit." She had the nerve to giggle.

Mike's stomach went to war with the sandwich. He'd never cared if he impressed a woman's father before. In fact, he hadn't met most of the fathers of the women he dated. Until now, he'd pointedly avoided them. Either that, or they had avoided him.

He reached up to pat where his tie should have been. He hadn't wanted it to dangle or blow around during his bike ride on the way there, so he had yanked it off as he was leaving. Now, when he wanted to make a good impression, he didn't feel completely dressed in a suit without a tie.

He tried to squelch the feeling of dread as he rose to his feet and nodded a stiff greeting. "Pastor Norbert."

Patty's father smiled warmly, but Mike's stomach wouldn't relax. "Hi, Mike, Patty. Sorry to disturb you, especially on this gorgeous day, but Cassandra Phillips is on the phone. She wants to talk to you about her daughter's Sunday school class. I told her you were on your break and couldn't come to the phone, but she started crying and said it was important she talk to you now. She said she's on her lunch break, too, and this is the only time she can call. I'm sorry about this. Would you mind?"

Patty sighed, stood, and turned to Mike. "I'm sorry, but I

know what she wants to talk about; I shouldn't be long. Do you mind?"

He rammed his hands into his pockets. "No, not at all. I don't mind."

He supposed it was better coming sooner than later. With Patty gone, this would be the perfect opportunity for her father to talk to him about all the time he was spending with her. He suspected that her father's sentiments about his character wouldn't be much different from Bruce's, and Mike couldn't blame him for that. He wouldn't be able to deny a word of why he shouldn't be in the vicinity of his sweet and precious daughter.

Mike struggled to prepare himself for the worst. He didn't want to take his hands out of his pockets, because he knew they were shaking. He didn't want to hear her father tell him to go away and not come back, because he didn't want to do that. Part of him told him to respect her father's wishes, but another part of him prepared to defend himself, even though he had no defense. If he didn't ever see Patty again, it would be like ripping out a piece of his soul. He couldn't do it.

Pastor Norbert checked his watch. "I wish I could stay out here and keep you company until Patty's done, but I have an appointment scheduled in two minutes. Maybe one day I'll have enough free time to join you and Patty out here for lunch. She tells me you make a great submarine sandwich."

Mike tried not to let his mouth hang open as Patty's father smiled, said a polite good-bye, and the two of them walked together toward the church. Mike heard them talking about the small child in question until they were out of earshot.

Mike sank to the bench. In the eyes of a righteous man like Patty's father, he was lowlife. Countless times he'd broken the law by drinking and driving, and the only thing that stopped him was being caught for the hit-and-run. Yet, even knowing that, Patty's father treated him as an equal, giving him a respect he didn't deserve.

He turned his head, meaning to watch them until they disappeared into the building, but a small movement caught his attention.

Patty's squirrel had arrived for its lunch. Mike studied it as it cautiously climbed up the side of the bench opposite to where he was sitting and then sat on the end, staring back.

Mike smiled. He was having a stare-down with a squirrel.

Very slowly, Mike lifted the paper bag containing the bread and reached inside. Inch by inch, the little squirrel tiptoed along the back of the park bench, until it was so close that Mike could reach out from where he was sitting and the little animal could take the food out of his hand.

He expected the squirrel to dart away with every small movement he made, but the squirrel remained still. He'd never moved so slowly in his life, but by using very slow movements, Mike managed to give the squirrel the pieces of bread, and it didn't run away.

The squirrel wasn't afraid of him. It was as if the little animal trusted him not to hurt it. In the same way, Patty's father had shown him in not so many words that he, too, trusted him.

Mike wondered what they knew that he didn't.

Deliberately, he kept his movements slow and steady, so as not to frighten Patty's squirrel. He held out another piece of bread, then kept perfectly still so the squirrel would again take it from his fingers.

Suddenly the squirrel darted away.

"Sorry I took so long."

Mike caught his breath, fumbled with the bag, and dropped it. The few remaining pieces of bread fell out onto the ground.

He looked up to see Patty standing behind the bench, both hands over her mouth, her shoulders shaking, and her eyes sparkling with glee. She'd never looked so beautiful.

"Don't say a word," he mumbled as he bent over to pick everything up.

"Me? Never."

"Yeah, right," he grumbled.

"I hope you don't mind, but after Daddy reminded me of your famous submarine sandwich creations, he got me started talking, and I think Daddy is going to join us for lunch sometime soon."

Mike smiled. Strangely, he didn't mind. In fact, he looked forward to it. "Not at all. Now finish your sandwich, because I'm not giving you your desert until you finish your lunch."

❧

Patricia sighed as she started the next load of laundry, wishing she could be outside in the sunshine on a beautiful spring day instead of downstairs doing laundry. Since she had been busy every night that week, Saturday afternoon was the only time left to do her housework.

In the background, Patricia thought she heard a noise. She pushed in the knob on the washing machine to turn it off, tilted her head, and sure enough, she heard the doorbell again.

She ran upstairs and peeked through the blinds to see Mike at the door.

"What are you doing here?"

He grinned. "Hi. Got a bucket?"

"A bucket?"

He jerked his thumb over his shoulder toward the driveway. "My car is dirty. I came to wash it."

"You came all this way to wash your car?"

"Patty, the dirt will damage the finish." He shucked off his backpack and pulled out a sponge.

"I could have given you a sponge. You didn't have to bring one, you know."

"Yes, I did. This is a special sponge, manufactured in particular for use on cars. I bought this at the car show a couple of years ago."

She stared at the sponge. It didn't look different from any other sponge. She didn't want to ask how much he paid for it. "It's really not that dirty that you had to come all this way. I washed it last weekend."

Mike froze. "What did you use?"

Patricia cringed. "Dish soap. That's what I use on my own car."

He squeezed his eyes shut for a second, then smiled tightly. "That's fine, but from now on, please let me wash it myself, okay? Would you mind if I came by every Saturday afternoon to do it?" He removed two brightly colored bottles from his backpack. The labels boldly stated a guarantee to preserve and protect the finish on fine cars.

She nodded woodenly and left Mike outside while she ran into the house for her bucket. The last thing she had left to do was wash the floors, but she owned only one bucket, which Mike was now using. "Want me to help? I don't have anything else to do."

He removed the sponge she stored in the bottom of the bucket and left it at the side of the driveway. "Nope. But you can keep me company, if you want."

He carefully rinsed the bucket out three times with the hose, then turned to the house. "Can I have some warm water? It works best with the stuff I brought."

"You bought that stuff at the car show, too, right?"

"Of course."

"I'm surprised you didn't buy a bucket at the car show."

He frowned, and his eyes narrowed. "Let's not get ridiculous."

She led him to the laundry sink where he filled the bucket with water exactly the right temperature, measured exactly two capfuls from each bottle into the water, and returned outside. He very diligently and tenderly scrubbed every square inch of the car, the whole time making sure not to touch it with his fingers until he had carefully washed away every speck properly, chatting very little as he worked.

When everything was cleaned to his satisfaction, he instructed her how to hose it down, two and three times in some places.

Patricia gritted her teeth. She didn't know how he trusted her to drive it when he didn't trust her to wash it.

After she hosed all the suds off, he double-checked it, then began to wipe it down with a special leather cloth.

"What are you doing? It's a warm day. The car will dry by itself."

He shook his head. "The water might spot. If you'll excuse me, I have to do this quickly."

Patricia couldn't stand it any more. She would show him spots.

"Oh, Mi-ike. . . ," she drawled.

He glanced over his shoulder while he continued to wipe the car. "Yes?"

She opened the hose full blast for a few seconds, catching him squarely in the center of his back, then ran into the house, laughing every step of the way. He would forgive her if she made something special for dessert.

૨ล

Mike guided Patty by the elbow as they entered Claude's church. Since she was the pastor's daughter at her own church, Mike understood Patty having strong ties there. For today, though, he wanted to be here. Claude's church was very similar to Patty's, except for one big difference.

Bruce wouldn't be here.

Mike realized he was placing Bruce in an awkward spot, but he couldn't help it. As Mike's probation officer, Mike's relationship with Bruce was supposed to be strictly professional, and seeing Bruce at church encroached on Bruce's private life. He knew cops and other law-enforcement professionals couldn't mix their private lives with those over whom they had authority, and Mike could well understand that. After all that had happened, nothing lessened his respect for Bruce's authority, but if things continued the way he wanted, the situation could become very complicated.

Patty had driven him to a few of the required AA meetings,

but he didn't want her to get involved, so he had now found other ways to get around. He knew some of the things said at the meetings would make her uncomfortable. Sometimes they made him uncomfortable, but they were things he needed to hear. He also had some thoughts of his own that he had shared at meetings that he didn't want Patty to hear.

The Monday meetings at Claude's house were closed to all except the specific people who had committed themselves to the intense twelve-step meeting. It was there that he could really let himself go, and he had.

Over the last three weeks, he'd shared some very ugly things about himself to the group, things that he had never told anyone. Having to sort himself out in an honest and open manner among people who shared the same addiction forced him to take a hard look at himself, and he saw many things he didn't like.

He would work on those things. God had forgiven him for them; Jesus died to erase them, but he had still done them. A lot of what the meetings were forcing the participants to do was to deal with things from the past so they could move on. Of course he could see the wisdom of doing so, but that didn't make it any easier to do.

He jolted himself out of his thoughts when Patty touched his arm. "Look, there's Claude. Let's go talk to him."

Her touch made him want more. He would have liked to slip his arm around her waist, or failing that, hold her hand while they walked around as strangers in a new setting, but he didn't think that was appropriate in a church.

He wanted to show Patty how special she was and how much she meant to him.

Seeing her at lunch every day was satisfying to some degree, but Mike wanted more. He wanted to date Patty properly, which brought him back to seeing Bruce in a non-professional setting.

Bruce had seen him at his worst; therefore, Bruce's opinion of him was understandably low. It was obvious to Mike that

Bruce wasn't pleased about the way he had been spending so much time with his sister; however, Mike was determined to rise above Bruce's perception of him. He fully intended to treat Patty with the respect and dignity she deserved, and, with Jesus in his heart, Mike also intended to prove himself as a decent human being in Bruce's eyes. However, Mike didn't want to think about proving himself to Patty's father, the pastor. The very thought struck fear in his heart.

As they reached the circle of people including Claude, Claude introduced them to the small group, not as acquaintances through AA, but as friends. Mike liked that.

He said little, since Patty seemed to be doing a good job of holding up her end of the conversation. He also wanted to follow her lead if anything personal came up.

He only half listened to the conversation concerning the upcoming ladies' function, and his attention wandered to other happenings in the large foyer. Some people milled around a table containing books and pamphlets, and almost everyone else in the room stood around, chatting in small groups.

A family of a man and woman and two small children were greeted heartily when they joined the group standing next to Mike and Patty. Mike really wasn't listening, but when he heard the words "broken arm" and "car accident," he stiffened from head to toe.

The new man in the group had a cast on his right arm, and Mike didn't want to listen, but the words "drunk driver" echoed in his brain.

Mike felt sick. If the man attended this church, he probably lived nearby, and it wasn't far from here that he had his accident. His lawyer told him the lone occupant of the vehicle, a man, only had a broken arm, and it wasn't too bad.

He couldn't help it. He completely ignored Patty talking to Claude's wife about their baby-sitting ministry and listened to the group next to him. It appeared the whole family hadn't been to church for four weeks because his wife, who had been staying home with the young children, had to go out and get a job while he wasn't working.

Four weeks. The time frame was too close for comfort.

Mike thought he might throw up.

He had to know.

Very gently, he tapped Patty on the shoulder and whispered in her ear that he had to have a quick word with the man in the group next to them. Sucking in a deep breath, Mike took two steps toward the group beside him.

Their conversation stopped.

The man with the cast on his arm blinked in surprise, then smiled. "You must be new here. Welcome to Faith Bible Fellowship. I'm Darryl. Sorry I can't shake your hand." Then he actually smiled.

Mike felt two inches tall.

"I'm Mike. Uh, Darryl, would you mind if I asked you something, uh, privately?"

Everyone in the group stared at him, but he couldn't find out what he wanted to know in front of them. It was hard enough only facing one person.

Darryl looked hesitant but then nodded and smiled to his wife and stepped to the side with Mike, where they were still close by, but out of that circle of conversation.

Mike forced himself to look into Darryl's face and kept his voice low as he spoke. "I couldn't help but overhear part of your conversation—that you were in a car accident involving a drunk driver. If you wouldn't mind me asking, what night was it, where was it, and was it a hit-and-run?"

Darryl smiled. "I don't know what to say. It was on May seventh, at Main and Furly Avenue. But it's okay. They caught the guy, so if you witnessed the accident, everything is all in motion. I'm just waiting for a court date to testify. It's nice of you to be concerned."

Mike's knees shook. He wished he could run away, but he couldn't.

He cleared his throat and rammed his hands into his pockets. He stared at the ground, because he couldn't look Darryl in the face as he spoke. "I'm afraid it's a little more complicated than that. You see, I was the drunk driver."

# ten

Patricia glanced to the side briefly while she listened to Claude's wife. The woman was a joy to speak with, full of love for the Lord, but Patricia really didn't want to leave Mike alone. Being her father's daughter, she was a key figure in the church and was very used to making conversation with relative strangers, as everyone always felt they knew her and spoke freely to her. As much as some people felt they knew her, she often didn't know them. Sometimes she didn't even know their names. All her life, the one-sided familiarity had helped her develop the art of holding a good conversation versus meaningless chitchat with people she didn't know very well.

She thought it nice to see Mike meet up with someone he knew. From the little he'd said of his usual friends, it didn't sound like any of them ever went near a church, so this was a pleasant surprise.

Patricia turned to glance at Mike as he spoke to his friend one more time, and as she did, she lost all track of the conversation she was supposed to be paying attention to. All the color had drained from Mike's face. He was staring at the floor while the other man was staring at Mike. Neither of them was talking.

"Claude, do you know that man Mike is talking to?"

"No, not really. I think his name is Darren or something like that."

"Excuse me," she said, and quickly walked to Mike.

"Mike? Are you okay? You don't look well."

He cleared his throat. "I'll be okay. Uh, if you wouldn't mind, I have to speak to Darryl, alone."

Patricia blinked and backed up a step. "Oh." She glanced back and forth between the two men. Neither of them appeared pleased to see the other, but she would respect Mike's request and leave them alone. "I'll be with Claude and Michelle."

She watched Mike and Darryl while she listened to Claude and his wife. Instead of talking, Mike pulled a pen out of his pocket, they exchanged phone numbers, and separated. Mike walked back toward her, so she quickly turned around, but first she watched Darryl as he rejoined his group. He said only a few words, and a woman in the group grasped Darryl's arm and stared wide-eyed at Mike's back.

Patricia stared up at Mike as he returned to her side.

"I don't want to talk about it," he muttered, then turned to Claude. "I think I need to go sit down. If you'll excuse us?" He nodded politely, and without another word, he led Patricia into the sanctuary where he chose seats in an empty section.

He sat in silence for a few minutes, staring straight ahead at nothing in particular as more people entered the large room. She was starting to worry in earnest when he finally spoke.

"That was the guy I hit."

A knot formed in the bottom of Patricia's stomach. Her first thought was that Claude had set Mike up for this meeting, but that wasn't fair to Claude. She knew Claude wouldn't do something like that without discussing it with Mike first. He also had said he didn't know the man, nor did Claude even get the man's name right.

She waited for Mike to continue, but he didn't. He continued to face the front in silence.

"Mike? If you want to leave, I'll understand."

He shook his head slightly but otherwise didn't move. "No. I need to be here." Very slowly, he turned to her and rested one hand on top of hers. "I'm sorry; I'm not being very good company."

"It's okay. I understand."

The lights lowered, the congregation stood, and the first song began.

Midway through the worship time, Mike recovered his composure. He actually sang the last song, which they had sung at Patty's church one of the times he was there, making it the only song familiar to him. When the pastor began his message, Patricia found herself only half concentrating. Most of her thoughts centered on Mike.

She felt sorry for him. It was true that his actions had caused someone to be injured, and it was his fault; but knowing him personally versus thinking of him as the unknown bad guy altered her perspective in what should have been a black-and-white case of right and wrong.

The difference was that instead of passing it off, Mike was actively trying to change. She wanted to say something to let him know that he had her support, but sitting in church in a public setting while they were supposed to be listening to the pastor's sermon was neither the time nor the place. The only thing she could think of to show Mike that she was on his side was to take Mike's hand and hold it.

He flinched in surprise when she grasped his hand, but Patricia didn't let that bother her, knowing the last thing Mike would have been expecting would be for her to touch him. He turned to her and raised his eyebrows in a silent question, and Patricia gave his hand a gentle squeeze as an answer. Mike smiled and held on for the rest of the service.

After the closing prayer, as Patricia hunched over to gather her purse from under her chair, the man Mike had been speaking to appeared beside them. Mike stood abruptly while she remained seated.

Darryl nodded down in greeting at Patricia and then turned toward Mike. "When you first came to me, you really sent me for a loop, but I've had a little time to let it sink in. I think I'm ready to talk to you now."

Mike looked down at her. "Would you mind? I won't be long."

She didn't know what she was going to do in a strange place, but Mike needed the time. "Take as long as you need."

Mike and Darryl left the sanctuary and turned the corner, going down the hallway to speak as privately as possible, leaving Patricia alone. Fortunately, Claude and Michelle sought her out, and when she told Claude that Mike had gone to talk to someone, they said they would stay with her until Mike returned.

They introduced her to a few of their friends, and before long, Mike joined them. Darryl and his family were nowhere to be seen.

She doubted Mike would want to make social conversation, so they politely excused themselves and left.

"How would you like to come to my place for lunch instead of going to a restaurant? Or if you want, I can just take you home, if you'd rather be alone."

He buckled his seat belt and turned to her. "It's going to be okay. Darryl and I had a good talk, but I have some serious thinking to do. In the meantime, lunch at your place sounds great."

It didn't take long, and they were soon at her house. "I hope you don't mind grilled cheese sandwiches. I know we have sandwiches every day, but I can't think of anything else to make that's fast, and I'm hungry."

"That sounds great. Can I help?"

"Sure. What do you want to do?"

He grinned. "Actually, I make grilled cheese sandwiches all the time, and I'm quite proficient at it. How about if you sit down, and I'll cook lunch?"

Patricia had never had a man make her lunch. It was an offer she couldn't refuse, so she sat.

Mike rolled up his sleeves. "Where's the frying pan?"

Patricia stood and pulled the frying pan out of the cupboard, laid it on the element, and sat back down.

Mike checked out the counter. "Where do you keep your bread?"

Patricia rose, walked across the kitchen to the breadbox, opened it, plunked the loaf in front of Mike, and sat back down.

"Where's the butter?"

She remained seated and pointed to the butter dish sitting on the counter, in what she thought was plain sight.

He removed the lid and looked inside the container. "Where's a knife?"

She pointed to the cutlery drawer.

"Got cheese?"

"I would think the fridge would be a good place to look."

He shrugged his shoulders. "Isn't it rude to rummage through someone else's fridge?"

Patricia got up again, opened the fridge, opened up the cheese compartment in the fridge door, handed it to him, and returned to the chair.

He cut a few slices of cheese and returned the remainder of the block to the wrapper.

"I just thought of something. What about—"

Patricia groaned and covered her face with her hands.

"French fries?"

She thought he should have guessed that frozen French fries were simply in the freezer. "Do you want me to make this lunch?"

He wiped his hands on his pants. "Naw. I'm almost done. But thanks for asking."

True to his word, soon the sandwiches were sizzling in the frying pan and a tray of fries was in the oven. After she pointed out the cupboard where the glasses and plates were stored, Mike poured the milk all by himself and served lunch. He hadn't asked if she had napkins, nor did she volunteer any, because that was the one thing she had run out of.

After lunch, rather than sit around, they went for a walk around the neighborhood, not talking about anything important, which was both relaxing and therapeutic.

For supper, Patricia laid everything out on the counter and did all the preparation, and Mike did the cooking.

Usually she attended the evening service, but today she didn't. Instead, they prayed together, asking for direction and guidance for Mike, and then she drove Mike home.

෨

"I missed you yesterday at church."

Patricia hit the Save key and nodded. "I went to a friend's church. I hope you didn't mind."

Her father snickered and patted her on the shoulder as he stood beside her, reading the screen she was working on. "Of course I don't mind. At times I worry that I'm tying you down too much. I like to see you get out with your friends."

Friends. She still wasn't sure what was happening between herself and Mike, but it wasn't just *friends*. All day Sunday, they hadn't talked about anything serious. She had given him plenty of opportunity to talk about meeting the man whom he had injured, but he hadn't. That was okay, too. Experience had taught her that people needed time for something like this to sink in before they could deal with it. What he needed right then was a friend, and being with him when he needed her was part of her ministry to Mike.

The biggest problem was that she was getting too attached to him. She didn't know when it happened, but he had become more than a ministry, and that wasn't in her plan. She wasn't sure how he felt about her, or how he still felt about his ex-fiancée. He had kissed her a couple of times, but that was at times when his emotions had gotten the best of him, and she really didn't know what was in his heart.

When everything should have been clearer, things were only getting cloudier.

Her father checked his watch. "I think your friend is going

to arrive any minute. I gather he's the same friend you went to the other church with."

"Mmm. . . ," she mumbled as she typed. She didn't know what to say to her father about Mike. Bruce's disapproval was already hanging over her head; she didn't want to hear the same from her father. Last night Colleen had phoned after the evening service to wonder where she was. After telling Colleen she had been with Mike all day, Colleen bombarded her with questions about a future with Mike that couldn't possibly happen.

Once Mike sorted himself out, he would move on to someone more in his social circle, someone who could keep up with his fast pace, and she wouldn't see him again.

She didn't want to think about that.

"Hi, Patty. You weren't outside, so I thought I'd find you here. Since it was my turn to bring lunch, I didn't think you'd take off on me."

She hit Save one more time, and they walked outside to the park bench where Mike emptied sandwiches, juice, and some cookies out of his backpack.

They paused for a short word of prayer and ate in silence. The squirrel came, and Patricia fed it in silence.

When only a few minutes of her lunch break remained, Mike finally spoke.

"I know what I'm going to do about Darryl."

"And what is that?"

"I phoned him this morning, and we had a long talk. His medical plan while he's off doesn't pay as much as his salary, so his wife, who was staying home to look after their two young kids, had to go and get a job. Even though the insurance paid to fix his car, it's never as good as new, and they only have one car. Worst of all, he's lost some of the strength and mobility in his arm permanently, which is bad because he's an auto mechanic. His boss is going to give him a job in the parts department, but that doesn't pay as much, and it's not what he wants to do. But he doesn't have a choice."

She wanted to tell Mike that it wasn't his fault, but that would have been a lie. It was his fault. He hadn't intended for this to happen, but that didn't alter the fact that it had.

"I read somewhere in the Bible, I forget where, that when a man takes something from someone else, he is to repay it all, plus a portion extra. I can't give him back the full strength of his arm, and he already told me he wouldn't take money, but I know what I'm going to do. I'm going to pay for him to take some kind of course while he's off work, so he can get a better job. It's not much, but it's the only thing I can think of."

"That's a wonderful idea. What did he say?"

"He said no, but I made him promise to talk it over with his wife. I don't see how they will be able to survive if they don't. I think he'll change his mind and accept in a couple of days. I also talked to Claude. He says that this kind of restitution is actually one of the steps that come later in the program. He said he knows how hard it is, but the only way to put all this behind me is to make peace with God, make peace with others, and then to make peace with myself."

Mike rested his elbows on his knees and clasped his hands, but he turned his head so he wasn't facing her as he continued. "Darryl said he forgave me, even before I told him that I would pay for a course. He said God forgave me, too, but I don't know if I can forgive myself. What if I hadn't ever met Darryl outside of court? What kind of mess would his life be? It's still not going to be easy for him. The man is a Christian. How could God have let something like this happen to him? And worst of all, I did it."

Patricia felt a lump in her throat. "I don't know. Sometimes bad things happen to good people. Sometimes we know the reason; sometimes we find out later. Most of the time, we'll only find those answers when we're with Jesus in God's Kingdom."

He turned, and the anguish in his face nearly brought tears to her eyes.

"I had better go," he mumbled. He swept the empty containers into his backpack and left before she could think of anything to say.

All afternoon Patricia worked with a heavy heart. Mike was overburdened with guilt, and he was obviously filled with remorse for what he had done. The man he'd hurt had forgiven him. God had forgiven him. Now if only he could forgive himself. She knew from experience that was often the hardest thing to do.

She pulled the AA pamphlet she had marked with the dates of the meetings at Claude's house out of her drawer. Tonight they would be working on step four—*Made a searching and fearless moral inventory of ourselves.* In the notes underneath, it stated Haggai 1:7—"This is what the Lord Almighty says, 'Give careful thought to your ways.' "

That would be a tough one for Mike. He was already looking carefully at himself, and Patricia didn't think he liked what he saw.

Blankly, she stared through the office door and down the hall leading to her father's office. Her father already knew Mike was one of Bruce's clients, but she didn't know how much Bruce had told him. According to Bruce, Mike wasn't the type of man her father or the church would approve of; however, Bruce only knew the old Mike. The Mike that Patricia knew was a new creation in God's sight, set apart and called by God to be one of His children.

For now, Mike needed the support of those around him, and most of all, he needed prayer more than she needed the approval of her father or her brother to continue to see Mike for what was no longer strictly ministry.

She closed her eyes, remembering the way Mike had kissed her. Even though she knew it wasn't a good idea, she had kissed him back, and she would have kissed him longer if he hadn't been the one to move away first. And that was wrong. She couldn't allow him to distract himself from building his relationship with God. How she felt about him had to come second.

Patricia walked into her father's office. "Daddy, I need to pray about something with you."

❧

Mike leaned his bike against the church wall and watched Patty trying to feed the squirrel.

It had taken a week, but Darryl had finally accepted his offer. For a few hours, he'd felt better about the way things were going, but then he'd gone to the step five meeting. *Admitted to God, to ourselves, and to another human being the exact nature of our wrongs.*

He'd done a lot of wrongs. He hadn't thought much about it before but, when he lumped together all the wrong things he'd done, he was a pitiful excuse for a human being.

Patty raised her head and waved when she saw him. The squirrel took off.

Mike cleared his throat and strode across the grass, forcing himself to smile, although he felt far from cheerful. When he reached her, he sat beside her on the bench.

"See?" she said brightly. "I scared Sally Squirrel all by myself today."

His stomach churned. At least it was one rotten thing that he hadn't personally done.

Today it was Patty's turn to bring lunch. Mike waited while she opened a small cooler on the ground beside her. She pulled out two submarine sandwiches, a container of potato salad, and a small cake, along with paper plates and plastic forks.

Mike blinked and stared at the cake. "Is it someone's birthday?"

"Nope. Do you like chocolate swirl?"

He looked down at the cake. "Uh, yes. Is it a holiday or something I've forgotten about?"

She shook her head. "No. I just wanted to give you something special."

A lump formed in his throat. He didn't deserve something special. He stared into the trees while he tried to think of something to say.

Her fingers touching his arm startled him. "I've been keeping track of what you're doing every Monday, and I know what you're thinking. God has forgiven you for everything you've done. All you have to do is lay everything at His feet. 'If we confess our sins, he is faithful and just and will forgive us our sins and cleanse us from all unrighteousness.' That's John 1:9."

At the meeting last night, Claude had quoted that same verse to him and to everyone there. He tried to respond, but couldn't.

"God has forgiven you, Mike. Now all you have to do is forgive yourself." Before she finished speaking, she unwrapped the subs and gave him one. When she closed her eyes, Mike did the same. "Heavenly Father, I thank You for this food, for this day, for the abundance of Your love that You pour down on us every day, and for Your Son, Jesus, Who died so that all our sins could be washed clean. Amen."

"Amen," he mumbled.

"Now let's talk about something fun. I want to go out tonight."

He blinked. "Uh huh. . ."

"When was the last time you've been to the aquarium?"

"The aquarium? You want to go with me?"

He couldn't believe it. She actually laughed. "Of course I do. Who did you think I meant?"

He didn't want to think about that. Even though she'd never talked about another man, he knew there had to be someone out there who was right for her—someone who was more suited to her and more worthy than him. Patty was pure and innocent, and he. . .wasn't. He should have been staying away from her. That she was his probation officer's sister made it worse. He didn't want to think about her being the pastor's daughter. Every day he was with her, she brought more joy to his soul. The days he couldn't see her, it felt like a part of him was missing.

Now, for the first time, it was Patty who was asking him to spend time with her, instead of the other way around. It was an offer he couldn't refuse.

Mike cleared his throat. "I haven't been to the aquarium since I was a kid."

"Then you're in for a treat. I discover something different every time I go, even though it doesn't change much from year to year."

"I'll be looking forward to it. But isn't tonight Bible study night?"

"Yes, but Gary and Melinda's kids came down with chicken pox yesterday, so their house is under quarantine for a while."

Mike shuddered at the thought. "What time do you want to go? Tell you what. Why don't you come over to my place and I'll cook dinner, and then we'll go."

She grinned, and Mike's heart flip-flopped in his chest. "Depends. Are you going to make grilled cheese sandwiches?"

He pressed one palm to his heart. "You wound me. I told you I'm an accomplished cook, and at my house I know where everything is."

"Well, praise the Lord for that! Name a time, and I'll be there."

He glanced at his wristwatch. He had enough food on hand so he wouldn't have to go shopping, but if Patty saw the way he kept his house, she'd never come back. "Six?"

"Six it is."

They shared the cake and he returned home, where he immediately began a flurry of housekeeping. The novelty of cleaning his house himself had worn off quickly, and as he worked, he grumbled to himself that the first thing he was going to do when he got a new job was to hire his house-keeper back.

After everything was picked up and the house was clean, he had a fast shower. When Patty arrived, he was ready.

# eleven

"Come on in. I hope you're hungry."

She smiled as she entered. "Yes, I am. Something smells good."

Mike patted himself on the back. They'd eaten together so often, he knew exactly what she liked. Patty was easy to please, so what he had prepared wasn't difficult. Many of the women he'd dated in the past would settle only for the most expensive, and the best, and certainly nothing home-cooked, especially by him. He had once interpreted it as sophistication. He now saw things differently.

What they had talked about last night at the meeting had to do not as much with the rotten things everyone had done but the motivations behind those things. For himself, it was self-centeredness that had driven him—not to succeed financially or have more than everyone else, because he already had more than he needed. Instead, after he sat down and really took a good hard look at himself, he saw everything he did was in some way related to feeding his ego and putting what he saw as his own needs, instead of the needs of others, first.

Starting today, he was going to put others first, beginning with Patty. He would work on the rest later.

Mike grinned. "Don't be too impressed. It's just a simple potato casserole recipe my housekeeper gave me because she felt sorry for me. I'm going to barbecue the steaks now that you're here. Want to come outside and talk to me, since everything else is done?"

He guided her through the house, smiling to himself at her reaction to his preparations. He had used the dining room table instead of the kitchen, and his setting included a tablecloth and

131

cloth napkins as well as a small vase of flowers he'd snipped from one of the bushes in the yard. All in all, considering he'd never cooked dinner for a woman before, he thought it looked rather romantic, and he was quite proud of himself.

The only thing not perfect was that since it was summer, it was still light outside. For an added touch, he would have liked to have had it slightly dark and to have either candles lit or the crystal chandelier on low.

She followed him into the kitchen where he uncovered the steaks which were marinating on the counter and transferred them to a plate. He bit back a smile as she not very discreetly checked out the whole kitchen. He'd carefully cleaned up after himself, including washing the bowls he'd used in his preparations, so nothing was out of place. He'd scrubbed the counters and sink with some kind of cleaner his housekeeper had stashed under the sink and then gone on to sanitize the whole house with it. Just using it made his eyes water, but it was worth it. Everything was now spotless, and the house was the cleanest it had been for a month.

He led her outside where his built-in gas barbecue was heated up and ready.

Patty shuffled her feet, then sat in one of the padded deck chairs. "There must be something I can do."

The steaks sizzled as they touched the hot grill. "Nope. I've got everything under control."

She folded her hands in her lap and sat straight in the chair, her back stiff as a board.

"Relax, Patty. You're my guest."

"Sorry."

To be honest with himself, he was as nervous as she was, except he had something to concentrate on, which was cooking. Before, when he was nervous, he offset it by having a drink in his hand, but that was no longer an option.

If he had had anything left in the house (which, of course, he didn't because Patty had dumped it all down the sink), his first impulse would have been to offer her a glass of wine. This was an old habit he would have to break.

It had been five weeks and six days since he'd had a drink, and this was the first time that neither he nor his guest drank while he entertained. Even as a child, before he was allowed to drink, he always saw that when his parents entertained, they always served alcohol, which was the socially acceptable thing to do. He felt the absence, as much by the breaking of a lifetime of habits as the addiction itself.

"I've got coffee ready in the kitchen. If you want a cup, help yourself." He flipped the steaks over. "I don't mind if you rummage through my fridge. I'd like to make you a cappuccino, but I can't leave this."

"It's okay. I can watch the barbecue."

"No way. I said I was going to cook dinner, and by that I meant that I'm going to do it all. Tell you what. I'll make that cappuccino after supper." He already knew exactly what flavoring she liked in it. He'd bought a jar of it last week, waiting for the day he would have the opportunity to use it. He'd also bought a can of spray whipped cream for the occasion, just in case.

For the time it took to cook the steaks, he told her a few jokes, and they shared some of his best and worst barbecue experiences over the years. She howled with laughter when he told her the story of when his neighbor's dog dug a hole under the fence, then somehow managed to knock over the plate of cooked meat when he went into the house to bring out the rest of the food. He had come back into the yard with his friends, ready to eat, and discovered the dog had eaten the wieners and left the steaks on the ground, untouched.

Today he didn't want to eat outside. He transferred the steaks to a plate and ushered Patty to the dining room. First he pulled out the chair for her, seated her properly, poured the coffee, and then began to place the food on the table.

She ran her fingers over the cloth napkins, then sniffed at

the flowers while he made a second trip back to the kitchen. Her eyes opened wide when he laid the potato casserole before her.

"Don't be so shocked. Not every single man lives on pizza and frozen dinners. It really was easy to make."

Next, he brought the dish of broccoli with cheese sauce out of the microwave.

"Don't tell me you made this yourself."

He grinned. "I'm good, but I'm not that good. The sauce is out of a bottle, but the broccoli is cooked to perfection."

Mike sat, tucked his napkin in his lap, and folded his hands on the table while she fiddled with her napkin.

He waited for a while, then spoke. "Shall we pray before it gets cold?"

Her cheeks turned pink, which he thought quite endearing.

After they paused for a word of prayer, instead of digging in, she continued to stare at everything.

"Don't be shy. Do you want me to eat some first to prove to you that you're not going to die of food poisoning?"

Her cheeks darkened again. "Sorry. I'm just so caught off guard by all this. You really did make this all by yourself. I expected something different."

"Did you expect me to be like the single guys on television—to buy takeout and put it on my own dishes and pretend I did it myself?"

Patty stared at the ground and said nothing.

"I made dessert, too."

"Boy. I don't know what to say. You went through so much trouble—just for me."

She didn't know the half of it. Preparing the food was nothing compared to cleaning up the house. It had been so bad, he would have died of embarrassment if she'd seen it. When his housekeeper came back, he would more fully appreciate all her hard work cleaning up after him.

He shrugged his shoulders. "It's not a big deal. Even if you hadn't come, I still had to eat. It was a nice change to be able to cook something special."

Her cheeks flushed, she lowered her chin, cautiously took a bite, paused, and then smiled. "This is really good. It would be perfect for a potluck at the church. Do you think I could have the recipe?"

Mike laughed. "No one has ever asked me for a recipe before, especially a woman. I guess so."

"No. Maybe I shouldn't. Next time there's a potluck, you can make this and bring it yourself."

Mike froze, his fork halfway to his mouth. "You're kidding, right?"

She smiled. "Wrong."

He'd never been to a potluck, and wasn't really sure what went on there. All he knew was that it had something to do with eating.

When they were done, he brought out the dessert.

Patty giggled. "This is Jell-O."

"Yes. And I boiled the water all by myself, too."

She tilted her head to examine it further. "And you were very artistic spraying on the whipped cream."

"I wish I had a cherry to put on top for a finishing touch, but my creativity only goes so far."

She glanced quickly at her watch. "I don't want to rush through this delectable treat, but if we're going to have time to walk through the aquarium without rushing, we're going to have to leave soon."

"Fine by me."

Soon they were in the car. Mike settled into the passenger seat and selected a CD while Patty drove. The novelty of Patty driving his car had worn off long ago, and he longed to be the one driving. Now the only time he got to sit behind the wheel was on Saturdays when he washed it while he cleaned the interior.

If he forced himself to think of something good, being

without his car had a few side benefits. Despite the fact that he had cashed in his membership at the gym, he was in great shape from biking for miles every day. He was also getting to know the people in his neighborhood. He was on a first-name basis with the clerk at the grocery store, because he could carry only what fit in his backpack and had to shop every few days instead of once a week like he used to. Since he was unemployed, he had plenty of time to strike up friendly conversations with other people in line rather than fretting away the time, anxious to be out the door.

Patty's voice broke him out of his thoughts. "Remember, since this was my idea, I'm paying."

Mike sighed. "Patty, don't do this to me."

"If you don't let me pay, I'm going to turn around right now, and I'll drop you off at home."

Mike grumbled his reply.

"Good," she said. "Here we are."

ða

Patricia smiled sweetly as she tucked her wallet back into her purse and patted it. "There. That wasn't so bad, was it?"

He mumbled something she couldn't quite make out, but she decided not to question him.

Since it was a weeknight and only a couple of hours until closing, the complex was nearly deserted, which was fine with her. It was comfortably quiet, with the only noise the bubbling of the aquariums and the low murmur of conversations from a few small groups of people in various places in the section they entered. The backlit aquariums in the dark room gave it a strange ambiance of privacy in a public setting.

They walked around the room slowly, enjoying the colorful fishes and other aquatic species on display.

As they stood watching a small display of starfish that weren't really doing anything, she felt the warmth of Mike's hand enclose hers. He gave it a little squeeze, and then didn't let go.

"This is really relaxing. You had a good idea. Thank you for suggesting this."

She nodded. "I really like it here. It doesn't change much, but it's just as fascinating every time I come. When I get home, I always think about setting up my own fish tank, but it's not the same."

They moved to the next display, a tank containing some strange creatures that must have been some kind of fish, but just seemed to sit at the bottom of the tank like rocks with eyes. Mike lowered his head for a closer look, and Patricia held back a snicker at his boyish curiosity.

No matter how close he stood to a tank, and no matter whether he examined the tank's occupants or read the blurb about each species, he didn't let go of her hand.

By the time they checked out a few more displays, they were the only people left in that section of the room. Patricia thought it would be a good time to get him talking.

"You haven't told me about your meeting last night. You always tell me something about what you did, but this time you haven't."

She felt him stiffen.

"Yeah, well, it's kind of a scary thing, having to start making a serious list of all the things you've messed up in your life. After the meeting, I couldn't sleep, so I made my list last night. Claude warned us not to get obsessive about it—just list the major stuff. Well, my list isn't very pretty."

Part of her wanted to assure him that it couldn't be that bad, but truthfully, she didn't know that it wasn't. She knew about his drinking and driving, and she wasn't stupid enough to think that the time he was arrested was the first time he did it. Bruce had also suspected that Mike had been under the influence of more than just alcohol at the time. It was a subject she didn't want to bring up. She also knew that he'd fled the scene of an accident. The thing that bothered her most was that he had been unfaithful to the woman he had promised to marry.

He continued to stare into the tank. "Claude gave us a list of verses. I think he meant to encourage us, but I'm still not sure about all this. Last night I read them so many times I think I've got them memorized."

"Memorizing Bible verses is not a bad thing, Mike. I've got a number of verses memorized."

"The main verse of the night was 'Therefore confess your sins to each other and pray for each other so that you may be healed.' I forget the reference. It's in the New Testament somewhere."

Patty smiled. She knew it was in the book of James but couldn't remember the exact reference. "Confession is good for the soul. Really."

"We're supposed to talk about this 'exact nature of our wrongs' thing with another person, and Claude said it's a good idea to do it with a clergy person. You're kind of a clergy person. You work for a church, and you've been to Bible college. You already know some of my list of wrongs. Do you think that counts?"

She could hear the anguish in his voice. Some people were able to freely admit when they messed up and confess their failings. Others were not. In her years of counseling, she'd dealt with both types. Mike obviously fit in the latter category. "Sure. I think that counts. Remember: Your life is not for me to judge. Whatever you've done, good or bad, is only between you and God, but it does help to talk about it."

He cleared his throat, but his words came out in a low rumble anyway. "You already know about the charges against me. And you know what happened with Robbie. I've obviously had a falling out with Dad, and of course Mom is even more disappointed in me. No one at work is going to miss me, because I haven't been the best manager. The list goes on. I've even been rotten to my housekeeper—when she was my housekeeper."

He stopped talking and looked up at the description of the species in the nearest tank, but he wasn't really reading the words. Patricia waited for him to continue.

"Everything I've done, it all comes down to thinking of myself first and not caring about the rights or feelings of others, even my family. I did whatever felt good at the time, without regard for anyone else. It didn't matter if I knew I was going to hurt them." He turned and stared blankly into the next aquarium. "I don't know why you put up with me, but you're always there." He swallowed hard. "You know what's really humbling? God pulled me out of the pit I was in and placed me with so many people who could help me before any more damage was done. Bruce. Claude." He turned around and, not releasing her hand, he reached up his other hand and ran his fingers down her cheek. "And most of all, you."

Patricia trembled at his touch. She had no idea that Claude's group would be doing something so deeply intense as this. Even in the strictest sessions, never had she pushed someone she was counseling to look at themselves so hard.

But then, she'd never counseled someone with such a powerful addiction, or who had made such a mess of his life. All she knew was that for those who applied themselves, with the help of God, the program worked.

Mike had displayed tremendous strength of character so far, especially since she understood the courage needed to honestly dig deep into oneself. He not only opened himself up to her and others, but he was moving past talking about it and was really doing something about it. Not many people could do that.

He prayed and read his Bible daily, trusting God completely for the guidance and instruction to be what God wanted him to be, and he was laying his life in God's hands, one day at a time.

"God loves you, Mike. With the sacrifice of Jesus, everything you've done is wiped clean."

He turned to her and smiled. "Yeah. I know. He really does, and it's great."

Patricia looked up at him, then closed her eyes and leaned her cheek into his palm.

Not only did God love Mike, Patricia knew that she loved him, too.

ⅈ⹀

Patricia checked her watch. Again.

She had laid out the hose, Mike's special sponge, and the bottles of his favorite cleaners in the driveway. She'd also bought an extra bucket, which she had also left outside.

But Mike wasn't there.

For all Mike's failings, one thing she had learned about him was that he was punctual. He arrived faithfully at the same time every day for lunch, and since he started coming on Saturdays to wash his car, he also arrived at the same time every week.

For the first time, he was half an hour late, and Patricia didn't know what to do. She'd phoned his house and gotten the answering machine, and he didn't answer his cell phone.

She knew that he was on his bike; therefore, if he had an accident, except for his helmet, he was unprotected.

Once more, she went into the house to phone him. Just as the answering machine clicked on, she heard a strange clunking noise on her porch. Patricia dropped the phone and ran to the door.

Mike had arrived. She opened her mouth to tell him how scared she'd been that something had happened to him, and then she would scold him for the same thing, but no words came out.

Something wasn't right. Instead of his jeans, he was wearing shorts. For some reason, he was wearing gloves with no fingers, he was breathing heavily, and he seemed taller than usual.

He panted as he spoke. "Sorry I'm late. It took me longer than I thought."

She first looked where he usually put his bike, but it wasn't there. Then she looked down at his feet. He was wearing inline skates.

She tipped her head back and looked up at him. He peeled the wrist guards off his hands, tossed them on the ground, then pulled the helmet off his head. A few locks of wet hair landed with a splat across his forehead. The rest of his hair hung in damp clumps, and a few drops of sweat dripped down his face. He swiped his arm across his forehead. "That was much harder than I thought it would be."

"You came all this way on those things?"

He let go a ragged sigh. "No. I had someone drop me off a few blocks from here, and I jumped through your neighbor's sprinkler just to look all sweaty. What do you think?"

"You don't have to be so sarcastic. It was an honest question."

He sank to sit on the bottom step, stretching his legs out and not making any effort to take the skates off his feet. "Sorry, I didn't mean to snap at you. I'm really hot and tired."

"I'll go get you some water."

She hadn't been gone long, but when she returned, instead of being on the bottom step where she left him, she found him stretched out, lying on the grass. He looked up at her from his position flat on his back. "Don't laugh. The grass is nice and cool."

"I'm not laughing. Just the opposite. I'm really quite amazed. It's quite a distance from here to your house. I wonder how many miles it is."

He lifted one foot in the air and began to undo the laces while still lying on his back. "I don't know. But it's too many miles to do this again. My ankles are killing me."

She looked to his car, parked in the middle of the driveway, ready to be washed, which was the reason he had come. "I bought another bucket, just for you to use for your car. I have to finish cleaning the house, so you do the car while I wash my floors, and then we can make supper."

"Sure." He pulled off the skates and thick wool socks and

added them to the pile beside the porch. He then padded bare-foot to the car, arched and stretched his back, bent to rub his ankles, and picked up the bucket.

Patricia left him alone to go to the basement and fill the bucket with exactly the right temperature water while she began to finish her housework.

He was still wiping the car by the time she was done, so Patricia headed into the kitchen to start making supper. She had expected him to walk in and offer to help, but when she had finished everything, including setting the table, and he still hadn't appeared, she headed outside to get him. She didn't make it past the living room.

Mike was lying on the couch, and he was snoring.

Out of curiosity, she picked up his cell phone that he had left on the coffee table. The battery was dead.

Very gently, she shook him. He opened one eye, then the other, and smiled lazily. "Huh?" he mumbled, "Did I fall asleep?"

"Yes. Now wake up. Supper is almost ready."

Slowly, he sat up, stretched, then rose and walked to the washroom, still barefoot, because the only footwear he had with him were his inline skates.

Patricia stared at the closed door. She'd spent the afternoon cleaning the house while Mike had washed the car. She had made supper while he made himself at home and had a nap.

It felt almost domestic, and she wasn't sure she liked it.

❧

Mike sat in his study at his desk. A few weeks ago they had done step six. *Were entirely ready to have God remove all these defects of character.* He'd found that step to be easy. After the time he'd spent with Patty at the aquarium talking about some of the things that made him tick, the good and the bad, he found it to be a real eye-opener to look at himself that way. Once he'd figured out the honest reasons why he had behaved so pathetically, he was more than ready to ask God to help him get rid of the garbage in his life.

Likewise, when the group had gone over step seven, *Humbly asked Him to remove our shortcomings*, that wasn't difficult, either. Not only was God the Creator of the universe, which included himself, God was also his Heavenly Father Who wanted to help him. All Mike had to do was pray honestly and seriously about it, and he knew that God would help him work on removing those shortcomings.

However, what they were doing this week was getting harder. Step eight said, *Made a list of all persons we had harmed, and became willing to make amends to them all.*

Mike held the pen in the air, but he wasn't quite ready to write any names yet. Making a list would be easy, but the caveat of the step was that for everyone he wrote down, he also had to be prepared to make amends to them.

He thought carefully of the people in his life whom he had harmed enough that he needed to make amends.

At first he was pleased with his completed list. It had only three names. For now, it was enough that he had made the list and was willing. He didn't want to think of next week when he would actually have to do it.

He folded the paper and tucked it into his Bible just as the doorbell rang.

It has been a long time since someone unexpectedly showed up at his door.

When he opened it, he made no effort to hide his smile.

# twelve

"Patty! Not that it isn't great to see you, but what are you doing here?"

Patricia smiled. It was almost word for word what she'd said so often lately that she'd lost count.

"I was just on my way home, and since it's payday, I don't feel like cooking. Would you like to join me for Sir Henry's?"

Mike groaned out loud, but Patricia could tell he was only fooling around. They'd been to Sir Henry's a number of times, and every time, Mike had enjoyed himself. It was close, the food was cheap, and despite Sir Henry's unusual decor, they enjoyed the atmosphere of the place. Most of all, they appreciated the privacy, because most of the times they'd been there, they were the only patrons eating inside.

"Sure. Just let me lock up."

Again, they were the only people inside while the line-up at the drive-thru window was consistently five cars long. They waited patiently while Henry finished taking an order at the window.

"What do you think Henry would do if one day we came through the drive-thru instead of coming inside?"

"Shhh!" she whispered. "Don't talk like that. It might be too hard on poor Henry's heart."

Mike laughed, which Patricia thought a lovely sound. He didn't laugh often enough, and she wondered how she could get him to laugh more often. Of course, going through the AA program with all its soul-searching intensity, and the fact that his court date was looming closer, might have had something to do with it.

They gave Henry their orders and were about to choose a

table when Patricia pointed to the display on the wall beside the cash register.

"Look. Henry has some new pictures."

Mike harumphed. "They're not new. He just moves them around on the wall so you think they're new."

"They're new."

Mike shook his head. "No, they're not. I've caught him switching."

"He was putting new ones up while he rearranged some old ones, that's all." Patricia pointed to what she thought was new since the last time they were there. It was a picture of all the pictures on the wall of the restaurant. "See? We would have remembered this one if we'd seen it before."

Mike's eyebrows raised. "He must be getting desperate."

"Either that, or he takes his camera everywhere."

While they waited, instead of sitting at a table, they walked around checking out all the pictures, something they'd never done before. They shared comments on many of them, especially the ones taken in various travel spots around the world.

Mike pointed to a photo of the Eiffel Tower. "What do you think of Paris as a honeymoon spot?"

Patricia opened her mouth, but no words came out. Up until recently, she'd never entertained the thought of a honeymoon, because she hadn't met a man she would have wanted to honeymoon with.

Mike smiled, and her heart went into overdrive. She wasn't supposed to be thinking of travel and honeymoon with Mike. She was supposed to be ministering to him as a favor to Bruce, and somewhere along the way, something very wrong had happened to her plan.

Fortunately, Henry called their number. She deliberately chose the table farthest away from the pictures of Paris, she changed the subject, and they ate in peace.

❧

Mike leaned his bike against the church wall and swiped

some of the wetness out of his hair. The dismal gray of the rainy day suited his mood.

Today was the day he had to start step nine. *Made direct amends to such people wherever possible, except when to do so would injure them or others.*

Since Patty wasn't sitting on the bench in the rain, he walked inside the building to join her at her desk.

She fumbled with the phone as she was hanging up with a call. "Mike! What a surprise! I didn't expect you today when it started raining."

He shrugged his shoulders. "I was halfway here when it started, so I figured I might as well come all the way. I was going to get wet anyway, no matter which direction I headed."

She smiled. "You're in luck. Since it wasn't raining when I was getting ready, I brought two sandwiches, and I just made fresh coffee."

For once, her cheeriness didn't affect him. "That's nice," he mumbled.

Her smile dropped. "What's wrong?"

He stared out the window at the rain, which was now coming down heavier. "I started to try making amends to the people I've hurt. I've already done what I can for Darryl. In the past few days, I've called my dad at least a half a dozen times and left messages for him to call me, and he hasn't. So I guess it's up to him now. The last one left is my ex-fiancée, but the number I have is out of service, and she's not listed in the phone book."

"Do you think she moved to another city? Or what if she got married and changed her name?"

"Don't know."

"I guess you don't know where she works?"

"Nope."

"What about a mutual friend?"

"Didn't have any."

"You mean you didn't know each other's friends?"

"Nope. Think about us. Except for the last little while, we wouldn't have had any mutual friends, either. Your friends are all nice Christian people, and they hang around mostly with other nice Christian people. My friends are all party-hardy drunks like I was. There wouldn't be any mutual friends because you don't have a thing in common with a single one of them. I'm not sure I have anything in common with them anymore."

"I'm sure that's not true."

Mike turned to her. "It is true. Did you know that I recently phoned the cops on my best friend? The night of the car show, my friends spent most of the night in the beer garden, and I went home. I phoned the cops because Wayne was going to drive after drinking all night. After I called, the cops were waiting for Wayne in the parking lot. Since he hadn't actually got in the car yet, they told him to take a cab home and pick up the car the next day, which he did. He hasn't talked to me since. First it was just my dad, now there's another person who won't talk to me. I'm trying to make things right. I really am."

"Sometimes when we ask people for forgiveness, it doesn't happen, and there's not much you can do about it. Whether or not it was received on earth, it was received in heaven."

"Yeah. That's what Claude said, too."

"Surely there's someone you can call to get her number."

He stared blankly into the rain again. "There is someone. Her best friend, Molly. I can't remember her last name, but I know where she works—if she still works there."

Patty's desk drawer squeaked open, and he heard a thump on the desktop. "There's one way to find out. Phone and ask."

Mike stared at the phone book. He could put it off, but the only person he would be hurting by not following through would be himself. He didn't know if Robbie could forgive him, but he wouldn't know if he didn't ask. In a way, if she refused to see him, it would make the whole thing easier.

He paged through and found the number for where Molly used to work and dialed. He noticed that Patty was shuffling papers, but her exaggerated motions indicated that she was trying too hard to look busy.

"Good morning, Quinlan Enterprises," the receptionist chirped.

Mike cleared his throat. "May I speak to Molly?"

"Molly? Sorry, she quit before the wedding."

"Do you have any idea how I can contact her?"

"Oh. Is this personal? She's here. One moment."

The phone clicked, and some music came on the line. Strangely, instead of the usual horrible canned music that businesses typically used for people on hold, it was a Christian artist he recognized. He was beginning to enjoy the song, when a male voice answered.

"Ken Quinlan."

"Sorry, I must have dialed the wrong extension. I'm looking for Molly."

He heard the phone getting passed. "Honey? It's for you. I don't know who it is."

Mike sucked in a deep breath.

Molly's voice came on the line. "Hello?"

"Hello, Molly. I don't know if you remember me. This is Mike Flannigan. I'm looking for Robbie, and I was wondering if you could give me her number."

Silence hung on the line, but it didn't last. "She's happily married; you leave her alone!" The phone shuffled again as it passed hands, but he could still hear Molly's voice. "Quick. Hang up."

The man didn't hang up, and Mike could hear him talking to Molly. "What are you doing? Who is it?"

"Remember I told you that before Robbie and Garrett got married, she was engaged to someone else, and the guy was a real creep? It's the creep."

Mike cringed, but it was nothing less than he deserved.

Molly had never liked him from the first time they met.

Ken spoke again. "Still, what does he want?"

Whoever was holding the phone covered the mouthpiece with his hand. Mike waited while the two of them argued, and although he heard the differences between the male and female voices, he considered it a blessing in disguise that he couldn't hear what was actually being said.

Ken's voice came back on the line. "Molly doesn't want to talk to you, Mike, but maybe you can tell me why you want to talk to Robbie."

"I've been doing a lot of thinking lately, and I wanted to tell her I'm sorry and wish her the best."

Mike's heart pounded while more silence hung over the line.

Finally, Ken spoke. "For some reason, I trust you. Tell you what. I'll do better than her phone number. I'll give you the address so you can do it in person. And just so you know, Robbie and Garrett are now the proud parents of one-month-old twins."

His hand shook, but Mike wrote down the address and directions to get there. In the background, he could hear Molly nattering her disbelief that Ken, who was apparently her husband, was going along with him.

Mike hung up.

"Well? How did it go?" Patty asked.

"I need to ask you a favor. Instead of sitting here for lunch, can we go to the mall? I need your help picking out a couple of baby gifts."

❧

Mike knocked on the door. He didn't have to recheck the address that Molly's husband had given him. He recognized Robbie's car in the driveway.

The door opened. A very big man holding a small baby stood in the doorway. "Mike." He nodded. "Molly told us you called."

Mike extended his hand, then pulled it back because

Robbie's husband needed both hands to hold the baby. Mike wasn't sure that Garrett wanted to shake hands anyway. After all, he could only guess what Robbie might have told her husband about him. He forced himself to smile. "You must be Garrett."

"Yes. We've met before."

Garrett stepped aside, allowing him to enter. Not too many men stood taller than Mike at six feet tall, but Garrett towered above him by a couple of inches. He had a husky build and a rugged complexion which hinted he worked outside. He appeared to be a man one would remember, but Mike didn't.

Thinking back during the time following the breakup with Robbie, he had fallen into a pit of heavy drug and alcohol abuse. Only recently could he admit to himself that he had suffered blackouts during that period of his life, and it bothered him. If that were the case, he didn't want to think of what he could have said or done, especially since Garrett wasn't exactly welcoming him with open arms.

The door closed behind him, and Mike suddenly felt very alone. Instead of just dropping him off, Patty had insisted on waiting for him in the car. He had found it comforting that even if she wasn't with him, she was watching. But now that the door was closed, the connection was broken, and he felt the loss.

"Robbie!" Garrett called. "You have a visitor."

Mike's stomach contorted as he laid the two gifts he'd brought on the coffee table and waited.

He had prayed about this moment more times than he could count, asking God to help him get proper closure to his relationship with Robbie, to give him strength and wisdom, and to help him be understanding of how much he'd hurt her if she didn't forgive him.

The more he thought about it, he also had prayed for Robbie, as he recognized that this wasn't going to be easy for her, either, but it was something they both probably needed to do.

Robbie appeared from around the corner, carrying another small baby. She was exactly as he remembered her, except her hair was a little shorter.

He cleared his throat, but his words still came out gravelly. "Hi. Congratulations on the twins. How have you been?"

"Fine. And you?"

"Fine."

They stood staring at each other.

Mike rammed his hands into his pockets. "I know there's no way I can ever make it up to you, but after all this time, I want to say I'm sorry for the way I treated you. You didn't deserve that. I'm really sorry."

She didn't say anything for awhile. Her eyes widened, and he could tell her mind was racing. "That's what you came here for? To say you're sorry?"

"Yes."

Silence hung in the air.

Robbie's eyes glistened, but she blinked it away. "I don't know what to say. Every once in awhile, I've prayed for you."

His throat clogged. "I think it worked. I got myself into a couple of big messes, but God has really blessed me through it all, helping me as I try to pick up the pieces."

They stared at each other for awhile.

Robbie shuffled the baby. "I don't know where my manners are. Please, sit down. Would you like a cup of coffee?"

All the tension drained from him, and he gave her a shaky smile. "Don't make coffee for me. I'm hyper enough right now without adding caffeine."

Robbie smiled and sat on the couch, and Garrett sat beside her. Mike took the single armchair across from them.

At first glance, Mike thought that Robbie and Garrett were very different from each other, but at the same time, they seemed perfect for each other. He was not only relieved that things were working out for her, but more than that, he was genuinely happy for her.

"I won't stay long. I know this is awkward for you, but it's something I needed to do, for a lot of reasons. Thanks for taking the time to see me like this."

"Actually, I never thought I would ever say this, but it's nice to see you again."

She actually smiled at him, and Mike knew that he had done the right thing. It released a bond he hadn't known had been weighing him down all this time.

"I know I handled myself badly, but we weren't right for each other. You two look so happy together, and now you've been blessed with children."

Robbie nodded. "I think we both knew it at the time. It's amazing how God can make things work, even when we can't see it at the time."

"Yes."

"So, are you married now, Mike?"

"No. There are a number of things I still have to work out before I can allow myself the privilege." He stood. "And speaking of that, I really should be going. I have a friend waiting for me outside in the car."

Garrett and Robbie stood as well. "Why don't you invite your friend in?"

While he felt infinitely better about Robbie and their past together, Mike didn't think it was a good idea to introduce the woman he loved to the woman he once said he would marry. "I really should be going. Maybe another time."

They walked him to the door where they both took note of Patty sitting in the car pretending to be reading a book. It was barely noticeable, but he saw Robbie and Garrett quickly exchange smiles.

"Tell you what," Robbie said. "We haven't decided on a date yet, but why don't you bring your friend to the baby dedication? That will also give us all a little more time for this to sink in. We'll let you know when it is."

Mike smiled. "That sounds like a good idea." He paused

before he walked away. "Thank you again for seeing me, Robbie. You have no idea how much this has meant to me."

"Same."

Mike turned and walked to the car where Patty was waiting for him. He slid into the passenger seat, but she didn't drive away. Without using a bookmark, she tossed her book into the backseat, grasped the steering wheel with both hands, and turned toward him.

"Well? How did it go?"

He hadn't expected it to go so well, nor had he expected to feel so good after it was over. Robbie hadn't come right out and said she had forgiven him, but he could tell she had, long ago. She'd even been praying for him, and the knowledge touched him deeply.

He knew Patty also had been praying for him, and he felt both humbled and blessed because of it. And now, added to his relief from the burden of seeing Robbie, Patty's beautiful smile almost made him lightheaded. He wanted to tell her he loved her, but there were still too many unknowns looming in his future.

He smiled. "It went great. I'll tell you all about it when we get home."

❧

Mike walked into the garage and stood still, staring unseeing at his car. For the first time in a long time, his car was in his own garage.

He had settled with the insurance company for the costs of the accident, but in addition to that, it was time for the renewal of his annual premium, and his rates had skyrocketed. After more than two months without an income, for the first time in his life, money was getting tight, and he really was having to watch where the money was going.

Patty often cajoled him about needing to save money, and he could no longer dispute her reasoning for not renewing the insurance when he couldn't drive. Patty had a car of her own to drive; she really didn't need his, and it was an expense he could no longer afford. Patty had driven the car into his garage and parked it permanently. Last night the insurance had expired at midnight.

Her friend Colleen had come to pick her up immediately after supper, and shortly after that, Claude had picked him up to go to the step ten meeting. *Continued to take personal inventory and when we were wrong promptly admitted it.*

Mike fiddled with the knot of his tie and left the garage. As always, God's timing was perfect. Bruce was due any minute to pick him up. This morning was his court appearance, where he was going to *promptly admit* to the judge how wrong he'd been.

# thirteen

Patricia entered the courtroom. Mike was already at his place in the front, sitting stoically beside a man whom she assumed was his lawyer. Bruce sat behind him in the front row. She quietly walked to the front and sat beside her brother.

"This is it, the big day," he whispered as she shuffled into the seat.

"Yes."

Patricia shuddered. She'd never been inside a courtroom before; she'd only seen court scenes on television. The real thing was far less dramatic. Everything was very formal. All the men at the front wore suits, including Mike. Even Bruce was wearing a suit, which was rare. She couldn't remember the last time she'd seen her brother in a suit, including church on Sundays.

Even from the back, Mike looked dashing in his suit. She had seen him in a suit only once before, on the day he'd shown up for lunch after what had been his last attempt to find a job before this court fiasco was behind him. At the time, she had laughed and teased him about trying to impress her father. She thought she was being very funny, but Mike hadn't laughed.

Unlike then, there was nothing funny now. This was the day they had been waiting for, the day that would be the catalyst to Mike's future.

He turned his head slightly, and she could see when he saw her out of the corner of his eye. He gave her a nervous smile, then turned his face forward and continued to sit stiffly with his hands folded on the table in front of him.

Mike's case was the first of the day. Still, the minutes dragged like hours.

"All rise!"

Everyone stood, the judge entered, and the court session began.

The way the clerk read the charges against Mike seemed so cold, and the sterile atmosphere in the courtroom made it worse. It was hard to believe that the Mike she knew and loved was the person who had behaved so callously only ten weeks ago. By the mighty hand of God in his life, he was a changed person. He had put his life in order and was moving forward again.

"And how does the defendant plead?" the judge asked.

Mike's lawyer stood. "My client pleads not guilty, your Honor."

Mike jumped to his feet. "Wait, that's not what I said. I'm guilty!"

The lawyer turned to him. "Sit down, Mr. Flannigan," he whispered firmly. "I'm following your father's instructions."

Mike didn't sit. He turned to the judge. "I plead guilty, your Honor."

The lawyer nudged him. "Stop it, Mike. You don't know what you're doing."

"I do know what I'm doing. I was wrong, it was my fault, and I'm guilty."

"But I can—"

The gavel sounded.

"Order!" the judge called with a firm voice. "Counsel, please approach the bench."

Patricia forced herself to breathe. She didn't want Mike to go to jail. She wished he could be let off. But he really was guilty and, in the eyes of the law, he deserved whatever the justice system handed down to him.

The entire courtroom was silent except for the lowered voices of the judge, the prosecuting attorney, and Mike's lawyer. She strained to hear what was being said, but only a low murmur of male voices was audible.

She watched Mike, alone at the front. The decision being made now would affect his whole future, yet he held himself bravely, sitting with his hands folded in front of him. Still, she could tell he was nervous, because as she looked to the side, she could see him tapping one foot. She'd never loved him more.

Both attorneys returned to their places.

The judge folded his hands in front of him and spoke to the courtroom. "Despite advice from his legal counsel, the defendant has pled guilty, and the record will remain as such. Prosecution has advised that the defendant had voluntarily made restitution to rectify the damage he has caused with the injured party, and this is admirable; however, this does not alter the fact that the defendant displayed a flagrant disregard for the law at the time of the infraction. Since this is a first offense, and knowing that the defendant has made restitution voluntarily, has been active in the AA program, and fully complied with the conditions and restrictions of his probation, I hereby sentence the defendant to prohibition from driving a motor vehicle for a period of one year, plus one hundred hours of community service."

He thunked the gavel on the stand and announced a thirty-minute recess before hearing the next case.

Everyone rose while the judge left the courtroom.

Patricia's heart pounded in her chest. God had indeed been merciful. He had spared Mike from a jail sentence.

Mike's lawyer thumped him on the back, and everyone turned to exit the courtroom.

As she also turned, she saw a gray-haired man who looked like an older version of Mike alone in the back of the courtroom. His eyes glimmered as he watched Mike leave the room, and as soon as Mike passed, he followed.

Patricia felt her eyes burn, but she blinked it back. His father had not had contact with him since he fired Mike, yet he had come to the trial. Mike hadn't known he was coming.

She turned to the front instead of filing out, leaving her the last person in the room. She hadn't known if praying for leniency was the right thing, so she'd prayed for God's will to be done and had then been ready to accept whatever sentence was handed down. She didn't know enough about how the system worked to know how Darryl told the prosecutor that Mike had tried to make things better for him, but he had, and she thanked God for the difference that fact had made in the judge's decision.

Bruce also must have submitted some kind of statement outlining Mike's progress under the terms and conditions of his bail and made comments and recommendations concerning Mike's progress and the projected outcome of his involvement with AA. He probably also reported his newfound faith in Jesus as his Savior, although she didn't know which would have more influence in the eyes of the legal system.

Now that it was over, she didn't know what would happen next. Of course Mike would be relieved and, now that there was no possibility of a jail sentence, she anticipated that he would have no difficulty getting a new job. Soon, all would be back to normal.

She wondered if "normal" would include her.

Patricia sighed. It was time to get on with life, whether or not it included Mike. She turned, glanced once more over her shoulder at the judge's desk and the witness stand, and left the room. Her footsteps echoed sharply on the tile floor until she exited through the heavy door, which she shut firmly behind her.

Many people lingered in the hall, most of whom she didn't recognize from Mike's session, and who must have been waiting to go in for the next case. Though the hall was crowded, two people stood out. Mike and his father. They stood to the side of the doorway leading into the courtroom, staring at each other in silence.

Patricia couldn't intrude. She wanted to say something to Mike about the favorable outcome of the judge's decision, but this was not the time. This was his time to make peace with his father.

Very quietly, Patricia turned the other way, left the building, and went back to work.

Fortunately, her father didn't question how things went in court. She wasn't ready to talk about it. Since she wouldn't be visiting Mike in jail, she didn't know when she would be seeing him. Also, Mike would probably be getting another job right away, so he would no longer be joining her for lunch every day.

If he had made peace with his father, that meant he would get his old job back, and in that case, his old ties would be mended, and he would be back in the society circles he was accustomed to, which didn't include lowly, unsophisticated pastor's daughters.

Patricia buried herself in her work, trying to keep her mind occupied with anything but what the future held for her—with or without Mike.

When lunchtime came, she went outside, the same as she did every other day. The squirrel joined her, but Mike didn't. Since he didn't come to scare it away, the squirrel ate every bit of bread that she offered while Patricia left her sandwich untouched. Just in case Mike tried to call the church and she wasn't there, she left her cell phone beside her on the bench, not caring if the ring would scare the squirrel.

It didn't ring.

When she returned from her break, she looked for a message on her desk, but her desk was exactly as she left it.

All afternoon, the phone was silent, and Mike did not rush in with an apology for being late. The entire afternoon passed, but when the clock struck five, she had no idea what she'd done all day. All she knew was that Mike hadn't come, nor had he tried to contact her.

She walked to the parking lot where only two cars remained, hers and her father's.

She stared at her little white economy compact. She had enjoyed driving Mike's sports car even though it didn't suit her personality or the lifestyle of a pastor's daughter to be driving such an expensive automobile. Now, having her own car back, it further emphasized the differences between herself and Mike.

An empty ache settled in her stomach. He had his car back. He probably had his old job back as well and had reestablished the ties to his family and the lifestyle with which he was comfortable. His absence today, and his lack of a phone call, confirmed what she had feared would happen after his court appearance.

He didn't need her anymore. It was over.

❧

Mike stood at Patty's door, fiddled with the knot in his tie, rang the doorbell, and waited.

When finally the door opened, Patty blinked and stared at his suit, then quickly glanced to the side where he usually parked his bike. It wasn't there. Her stunned expression made him smile.

"May I come in?"

"Uh. . .yes. . .of course. . ." She stood to the side to allow him entry. "How did you get here?"

"Bruce dropped me off."

She checked her watch. "You were at the courthouse all day?"

Mike shook his head. His stomach knotted as he began to think that perhaps coming here like this wasn't such a great idea, especially when she found out what he'd done. "No. I had some errands to run, and Bruce drove me around. I asked him if he wouldn't mind dropping me off here. I hope you don't mind."

"Of course I don't mind."

"Actually, I was hoping that we could go out for dinner. Someplace quiet, where we could talk."

"Talk?" She backed up, which he thought rather strange and not like Patty.

"Yes. I wanted to thank you for all you've done for me. I want to take you out for dinner."

"Because it's over?"

He sighed, and all the tension left him. It had been a long and difficult ten weeks, and the wait was arduous, but it was finally over. The sentence was light and very much in his favor, if he handled himself properly.

"Yes," he said. "Because it's over."

He had tied up almost all the loose ends in his life. He'd done what he had promised and paid for Darryl's course. He'd had a long talk with his father and made things right there. He had arranged some of the hours of service for his sentence. He'd also made some very difficult decisions regarding the direction of his future.

There was only one thing he had to do now, and that was settle everything with Patty.

"I don't know. I'm really tired." She looked up at him. Her eyes glimmered, and she turned her head so she wasn't facing him.

For a second Mike thought maybe she was going to cry. Either that or she was overtired and was having some kind of female reaction related to the relief from the recent days of constant stress during the long process leading up to his court case. Now that it was finished, he, also, was exhausted—but excited at the same time. He could finally make some plans.

Patty looked up at him with bloodshot eyes. A pang of guilt shot through him. He didn't feel half as bad as she looked, and he felt bad that his predicament had taken such a toll on her. She didn't deserve to be saddled with his burdens. He hadn't slept well last night, but it hadn't occurred to him until now that perhaps Patty hadn't, either. Still, no matter how tired he was, he couldn't let the day end without telling her what he had decided. He didn't want her to find out from Bruce tomorrow, so he had to tell her himself, today.

He stepped forward and took her hands in his. "Please? We can still be home early, in plenty of time for you to get a good night's sleep for work tomorrow."

She blinked fast a few times and faced him again. "Okay."

"We'll go somewhere simple, and cheap, just for you." He smiled, hoping his little attempt to cheer her up would help, but instead, she stiffened and pulled her hands out of his.

She picked up her purse from the floor and locked the door as they left. He suggested Sir Henry's Fish and Chip Palace, but instead of the reaction he hoped for, she simply nodded and turned in the right direction.

He tried to get a conversation started, but her response was less than enthusiastic. Now he worried more than ever that perhaps this wasn't the best timing.

The same as every other time they were at Sir Henry's, they were the only patrons inside, but the drive-thru lineup went on forever. Today, that suited him just fine. Henry was busy, so they had the place to themselves.

They placed their order, and Mike led her to a table. She didn't say a word, so Mike gathered his nerve and decided to simply start at the beginning.

"I talked to your father today."

"My father? When were you at the church? I was there all day and didn't see you."

"I didn't actually go there, I talked to him on the phone. You didn't answer the phone when I called, so I figured you must have been outside with your chipmunk."

She turned her head and stared out the window. "Yes, I managed to feed him the whole piece of bread for the first time in a long time."

His gut clenched. He was hoping she would say that she

had missed him, but she didn't. Even a comeback that it really was a squirrel, not a chipmunk, would have been preferable to her bland response.

"Daddy never told me you called."

"Now don't be mad at him. I told him I wanted to tell you myself. Part of my community service is going to be spending a few sessions talking with the youth group and the youth groups from a few other churches about drugs and alcohol."

She turned and smiled at him, her first smile in a long time. He couldn't help but smile back.

"That's great, Mike. I'm sure they'll listen to you knowing how much you've been through."

"Yeah. Bruce thinks it's going to be a great ministry to the youth. He said they'd really listen to me, hearing it from someone who has experienced firsthand where it can lead."

"Yes, and you'll also have some stern warnings about drinking and driving."

He nodded. "You got that right."

"Especially when they see your car, they'll see the sacrifice it is to not be able to drive it."

"Yes, I'm sure they'll see it often, too. Bob Johnson is going to have lots of fun with it."

"Bob Johnson? You mean Billy Johnson's dad? I don't understand."

"Yup. Bob Johnson. He bought it this afternoon. I sold it."

She covered her mouth with both hands and gasped. "You sold your car?!"

He shrugged his shoulders. "Yeah. Well, I can't drive for another ten months."

"But ten months isn't that long! Surely you could have waited for ten months!"

Mike turned his head and stared out the window. He knew how much she enjoyed driving the car, and he wished he could have let her continue, but he didn't have a choice. "I needed the money," he mumbled. "Bruce happened to mention how much Bob liked the car, being a collector's edition, and he made me an offer I couldn't refuse. I needed the money to pay the college."

"Oh, Mike, I didn't know! If you could have held on for just a little while longer, I'm sure you'll have no problem getting a job now that you know you won't be going to jail. I could have loaned you something if you were running that low."

Henry plunked the tray of food in front of them. "You two looked lost in conversation, and you didn't come when I called your number. Enjoy it before it gets cold." He turned and hurried back to the drive-thru window.

"I won't take a loan from you, Patty. I wouldn't be able to pay it back for at least a year, and I can't do that to you." He reached over the table and covered her hands with his. "Come on. Let's pray." He closed his eyes and bowed his head. "Dear Lord, thank You for Your blessings, for Your kindness, and Your mercy. Thank You especially for this day, the decision of my court case, and I pray for Your will to be done in whatever the future holds."

"Amen," she mumbled.

Mike took a huge bite of Sir Henry's special recipe. He had skipped lunch, and he was starving. Fish had never tasted so good.

"What about your father? I thought you talked to your father."

He swallowed and sipped his drink to wash it down to allow himself to speak. "I'm not borrowing the money from my father. For once, I have to be able to do something myself without my father behind me picking up the pieces."

"Didn't he give you your job back?"

"Not exactly. He did give me a job, but not the same one as I left. The job he gave me doesn't pay very well."

Her eyes widened, and the pity in them made him lose his appetite. The last thing he wanted was for Patty to feel sorry for him.

"This isn't coming out right." He covered his face with his palms, then rested his hands in his lap. "Patty, I wanted tonight to be special because I'm not going to be able to see you very much for a very long time."

Her eyes opened wide and she froze, with a lone French fry dangling from her fingers.

"You see, I'm going back to school."

"School?"

"Dad wants to retire in a few years, and I have no real management or business skills. I have to be able to take over the reins of the company and run it successfully. When I paid for Darryl's course, I also signed up for a business management course for myself. It starts in two weeks, and I should graduate next spring. I'll be going to school full-time and working part-time evenings and weekends, starting at the bottom instead of the top this time. I'm going to be working in the warehouse, driving the forklift and doing the stock. While I'm learning how to run a company in the day-time, I'll be seeing how it really works in a practical application at night."

"You're going to be a stock boy?"

He nodded. "And I have to squeeze that in around my sentence of the community service, so that cuts into the time I can actually earn a salary, to say nothing of studying."

"Oh."

He wanted to reach over the table and hold her hands, but he could feel the grease from the fries on his fingers, so he didn't touch her. "So I'm not going to have much time to see you."

She gulped. "Oh," she muttered.

"I also talked about something else with your father."

She stared at him blankly.

Mike cleared his throat. "I asked if, as a pastor, he'd mind having a son-in-law with a criminal record."

"Son-in. . ." Her face paled.

Mike sucked in a deep breath. "Today closes the book of

my past sins. You've helped me through it more than I can say. You've been such a prayer warrior for me. You've supported me when I was weak, and I want you to know how much that means to me. In a way, you've been my mentor, but I don't want you to be my mentor any more. I want you to be my best friend, my help-mate, my partner."

He wiped his hands on his napkin, stood, then walked around the table. Once he was in front of her, he sank down on one knee, pulled the squashed French fry out of her fingers, and covered her hand with both of his. "I love you, Patty. I know this is asking a lot, but I'd like you to think about the possibility of getting married after I graduate. I know it's going to be hard, but knowing you're there for me at the end will make it all worthwhile."

Her eyes glistened, welled up, and tears streamed down her cheeks. "I love you, too," she sniffled. "Of course I'll marry you."

Joy like he'd never experienced surged through him. Mike stood, pulled Patty to her feet, and wrapped his arms around her. He buried his face in her hair and inhaled the sweet fragrance of her apple-scented shampoo, doing his best to ignore the heavy smell of the deep fryer that always permeated Sir Henry's. He thought his heart would burst when she wrapped her arms around his back and squeezed.

The loud snort of Henry blowing his nose echoed behind him.

"That's so beautiful," Henry mumbled, and blew his nose again. "Can I take your picture? No one has ever proposed in my restaurant before."

Patty sniffled, they separated, and she looked up at him. Her beautiful smile almost made him lightheaded. "Do you mind?" she asked.

The woman he loved just said she would be his wife. He wouldn't have minded if Henry wanted to film a movie as long as he got a copy so he could look at it when the pressure of the next year threatened to overwhelm him.

He turned to Henry. "Only if you'll come to the wedding."

The flash of the camera was Henry's reply.

# epilogue

Patricia watched the tears form in her father's eyes. "I now pronounce you man and wife. You may kiss your bride."

Mike lifted her veil and kissed her, but instead of the short peck they'd discussed at the rehearsal, he embraced her and kissed her fully. She leaned into her new husband and kissed him back in equal measure, until she thought her knees would give out. The sound of her father clearing his throat brought them both to their senses.

Her father wiped his eyes, cleared his throat once more, and addressed their guests in the church, which was packed with standing room only.

"Before Mike and Patty walk down the aisle for the first time as Mr. and Mrs. Michael R. Flannigan, Jr., I want to read this Scripture that Mike requested. Psalm 103, verses 1–4.

> *"Praise the Lord, O my soul;*
> *all my inmost being, praise his holy name.*
> *"Praise the Lord, O my soul,*
> *and forget not all His benefits.*
> *"He forgives all my sins and heals all my diseases;*
> *"He redeems my life from the pit and crowns me*
> *with love and compassion."*

Patricia smiled and squeezed Mike's hand. The next six months were going to be difficult; however, after two months of struggling to see each other between school, his job, and his community service requirements, they discovered that his suspended driver's license made it too difficult for them to see each other. So they just gave up and got married earlier

168

than they had planned.

Autumn was a fine time for a wedding, and they didn't care that they couldn't take their honeymoon until after his graduation, although she did have a feeling that, when Monday came, he wouldn't exactly be in the mood for his first class.

He smiled back, squeezed her hand, and they began their walk down the aisle. Joy radiated from him, so unlike the first day she'd shown up on his doorstep.

He had changed and grown so much since they met, not only as a Christian, but also as a person.

After his court case, he had worked hard on the last two steps in the AA program, which were *Sought through prayer and meditation to improve our conscious contact with God as we understood Him, praying only for knowledge of His will for us and the power to carry that out,* and *Having had a spiritual awakening as a result of these steps, we tried to carry this message to alcoholics, and to practice these principles in all our affairs.*

He hadn't come to know Jesus in the same way she had, but his love for Jesus was evident in every part of his life, both at school and on the job for his dad, and she loved him more every day because of it. He'd made new friends in the church, and he'd developed a wonderful ministry with the youth group, who loved him.

The church door opened to the parking lot, where four hundred people waited to shower them with rice. Instead of small bags, many members of the youth group held boxes.

A number of rice boxes began to shake, the sound increasing in volume. When she cringed, Mike leaned down to whisper in her ear. "Don't worry, I knew what they were going to do. I have a plan."

Patricia turned to her new husband. "You're kidding, right?"

Mike grinned. "Wrong."

They began their walk through the crowd of well-wishers, until they were at the section where the youth group was congregated. A split second before the torrent of rice poured upon them, Mike reached into his sleeve, whipped out a small umbrella, and opened it with a flick of his thumb. His free arm wrapped around her waist and pulled her close as the rice thundered onto the umbrella, slid down, and within a few seconds covered their feet.

Patricia raised herself to her tiptoes through the rice, wrapped her hands around his neck, and gave him a quick kiss, at which the crowd hooted.

"My hero," she whispered.

Mike grinned. "Yeah?"

She gazed into his smiling eyes, eyes that radiated with pure joy. God really had pulled Mike from the pit. After intense soul-searching, some hard work, and much prayer, everything in Mike's life was fitting into place. His future was set with his ministry, he was working toward high goals for his career, and within a couple of years, they would start a family. He'd met all the challenges and obstacles in his way first with prayer and then with courage and diligence.

Patricia grinned back. "Yes. You really are my hero."

And she wouldn't have it any other way.

# A Letter To Our Readers

Dear Reader:

In order that we might better contribute to your reading enjoyment, we would appreciate your taking a few minutes to respond to the following questions. We welcome your comments and read each form and letter we receive. When completed, please return to the following:

Rebecca Germany, Fiction Editor
Heartsong Presents
PO Box 719
Uhrichsville, Ohio 44683

1. Did you enjoy reading *My Name Is Mike?*
   ☐ Very much. I would like to see more books
      by this author!
   ☐ Moderately
      I would have enjoyed it more if _____
      _____
      _____

2. Are you a member of **Heartsong Presents**? Yes ☐ No ☐
   If no, where did you purchase this book? _____
   _____

3. How would you rate, on a scale from 1 (poor) to 5 (superior), the cover design? _____

4. On a scale from 1 (poor) to 10 (superior), please rate the following elements.

   _____ Heroine     _____ Plot

   _____ Hero        _____ Inspirational theme

   _____ Setting     _____ Secondary characters

5. These characters were special because_____

_____

_____

6. How has this book inspired your life?_____

_____

_____

7. What settings would you like to see covered in future
   **Heartsong Presents** books?_____

_____

_____

8. What are some inspirational themes you would like to see
   treated in future books?_____

_____

_____

9. Would you be interested in reading other **Heartsong
   Presents** titles?          Yes ❑          No ❑

10. Please check your age range:
    ❑ Under 18        ❑ 18-24        ❑ 25-34
    ❑ 35-45           ❑ 46-55        ❑ Over 55

11. How many hours per week do you read?_____

Name _____

Occupation _____

Address _____

City _____ State _____ Zip _____

# *Gift* OF LOVE

Gifts have become an expected
part of the Christmas tradition.
But a gift given without love is wasted. . . .

Four young couples have a lot to learn about love over
the short holiday season. Join their Christmas celebrations
as you unwrap a new gift in each novella. The *Gift of Love*
will be yours to cherish with each story of love and romance.

## paperback, 464 pages, 5 ³⁄₁₆" x 8"

❤ ❤ ❤ ❤ ❤ ❤ ❤ ❤ ❤ ❤ ❤ ❤ ❤ ❤ ❤

❤ ❤ ❤ ❤ ❤ ❤ ❤ ❤ ❤ ❤ ❤ ❤ ❤ ❤ ❤

# Hearts♥ng

Any 12
Heartsong
Presents titles
for only
$26.95 *

## CONTEMPORARY
## ROMANCE IS CHEAPER
## BY THE DOZEN!

**Buy any assortment of twelve**
*Heartsong Presents* titles and
save 25% off of the already
discounted price of $2.95 each!

*plus $2.00 shipping and handling per order
and sales tax where applicable.

## HEARTSONG PRESENTS *TITLES AVAILABLE NOW:*

(If ordering from this page, please remember to include it with the order form.)

# ·····Presents·····

## Great Inspirational Romance at a Great Price!

**Heartsong Presents** books are inspirational romances in contemporary and historical settings, designed to give you an enjoyable, spirit-lifting reading experience. You can choose wonderfully written titles from some of today's best authors like Veda Boyd Jones, Yvonne Lehman, Tracie Peterson, Andrea Boeshaar, and many others.

*When ordering quantities less than twelve, above titles are $2.95 each.*
*Not all titles may be available at time of order.*

# Hearts♥ng Presents
## *Love Stories*
## *Are Rated G!*

That's for godly, gratifying, and of course, great! If you love a thrilling love story, but don't appreciate the sordidness of some popular paperback romances, **Heartsong Presents** is for you. In fact, **Heartsong Presents** is the *only inspirational romance book club* featuring love stories where Christian faith is the primary ingredient in a marriage relationship.

Sign up today to receive your first set of four, never before published Christian romances. Send no money now; you will receive a bill with the first shipment. You may cancel at any time without obligation, and if you aren't completely satisfied with any selection, you may return the books for an immediate refund!

Imagine. . .four new romances every four weeks—two historical, two contemporary—with men and women like you who long to meet the one God has chosen as the love of their lives. . . all for the low price of $9.97 postpaid.

*To join, simply complete the coupon below and mail to the address provided.* **Heartsong Presents** romances are rated G for another reason: They'll arrive *Godspeed!*

---